Contents

Contents

You will also enjoy Alan Robbins's
first interactive mystery novel

A CALL FOR MURDER

"Interesting and innovative...A unique
thriller in which the reader can choose the
course of detection to be taken."
> Bob Ellison
> *Los Angeles Daily News*

"A clever idea...Sure to spark competition
among serious mystery fans."
> Toby Bromberg
> *Rave Reviews*

Also by Alan Robbins:

PUZZICLES*

MORE PUZZICLES*

A CALL FOR MURDER*

CUT AND CONSTRUCT YOUR OWN BRONTO-
 SAURUS*

ON THE TRAIL OF BLOOD

THE SECRET OF THE GOLD JAGUAR

GRANDMA'S PANTRY COOKBOOK (with Trudy
 Smoke)

*Published by Ballantine Books

MURDER IN A LOCKED BOX

Alan Robbins

BALLANTINE BOOKS • NEW YORK

Library of Congress Catalog Card Number: 89-90727

ISBN 0-345-35465-6

Printed in Canada

First Edition: August 1989

It was the greatest trick of the season. A triple escape from a tied sack inside a nailed crate within a padlocked trunk that is filled with water.

The Great Baldini would perform his great escape at the annual convention of the Society of Conjurers and Magicians and finally win the respect of his colleagues. But something went wrong during the practice run. And when a frantic assistant finally opened all the ropes and locks, there was Baldini still trapped inside, drowned. A tragic accident during a dangerous stunt, the police conclude.

You, of course, think otherwise.

But can you support your hunch and determine who killed the escape artist? Was it his jealous rival, his angry ex-wife, his nervous accountant? And how was the crime committed? Getting *out* of locked boxes was easy. But to murder Baldini, someone had to break *in*!

Your only chance is to call the suspects and witnesses at the hotel rooms where they're staying for the convention, to follow the trail of clues and hints. Ten phone calls can solve the crime—but they must be the right ones or the murderer will vanish faster than you can say abracadaver.

How to Read This Book

The pages immediately after the Introduction contain a listing of all the magicians staying at the hotel for the annual convention.

When you've finished reading the Introduction, decide who you want to call first and then consult the list. The two-digit number shown there is both the room and phone number. You can make the call by looking up that two-digit number in the upper corners of the pages throughout the rest of the book.

After each call, return to the list and decide who to call next. Listen carefully to what people tell you in each conversation, then try to make further calls that will elicit more clues. But watch out for lies, false leads, and misdirections—since the members of the Society are notoriously suspicious of each other.

It is possible to solve this mystery in only ten phone calls, but they have to be the right ones. It may help to write notes on the listing, to keep track of which numbers you call and in what order. When you think you have a solution, call Madame Pollidor at number 99 and find out how well you did!

Introduction

"The Great Baldini is gone!" says the woman at the other end of the telephone line.

"Did somebody steal it from a museum?" you ask, hoping for a mystery to break the boredom of the hotel room.

"I mean," she continues, speaking slowly to get in sync with your slow wit, "that The Great Baldini is dead!"

"Oh! Was it an endangered species?" you say, still not quite getting the gist of the tragedy.

"Dear, dear," she says sadly, "you don't know who The Great Baldini was? But aren't you a magician, too?"

"No, I'm a writer."

"Newspaper?"

"Mystery."

"Then why are you staying here at the hotel during the annual SCAM convention?"

"The what?"

"The Society of Conjurers and Magicians?"

"Oh, that. I'm just sitting in for my cousin Edgar. He was the magician in the family. I was the perennial dupe."

"Oh, you're Edgar Poole's cousin. Edgar is one of the

best of the amateurs in our Society. He couldn't make it this year?"

"No, and he asked me to take his place and tell him what went on."

"No wonder the name Baldini doesn't mean anything to you. Well, you'll have quite a story to tell him, dear. The Great Baldini was the world's greatest escape artist. At least that's what his posters claimed."

"Like Houdini?"

"He certainly wanted to be. But he could never quite win the respect of his colleagues. From what I hear, he was a bit of the rat. In any case, he came up with a new act last year, trying to finally gain the esteem of the other magicians. It was called the Triple Water Escape. He was handcuffed and tied into a sack. Then the sack was put into a crate which was nailed closed and tied with heavy rope. Then the crate was lowered into a trunk filled with water and the lid of the trunk padlocked. He was out in ten seconds, I've heard."

"Wow!"

"Of course no one had actually seen the trick. That's all just hearsay. Call Simon Penn if you want to get the details about it. He writes our Society newsletter. Everyone tells Simon what they're doing. Anyway, Baldini was going to introduce the trick at the convention Ball tonight. It's a showplace for a lot of new stunts. But something went wrong."

"Something...like what?"

"No one knows. He had reserved the stage downstairs for a practice run this morning. He was going through the whole routine exactly as if there was an audience, just to get everything right. But he never escaped."

"Did he vanish...*poof*?"

"No, he drowned...*glub*. His assistant found him floating belly-up in the water. The police were here at seven-thirty this morning. Didn't you hear the commotion?"

"I was still asleep. Are the police still here?"

"I think they left. There wasn't anything for them to do. It was just a terrible accident. But they told us all to wait in our rooms until their final report is filed."

"Are you sure it was an accident?"

"Listen, dear, I'm just a clairvoyant, not a detective. But I do know that all escapes are dangerous. A tremendous amount of exertion is needed, especially in Baldini's case since it was done underwater."

"Did anyone have it in for Baldini?"

"Well, he did have his enemies. He was ambitious, even ruthless. But I suppose an escape artist has to be. He and Stu Stuben were having a well-publicized quarrel. And his ex-wife, Lady Dierdre, was suing him for alimony. Of course, you never know if these battles are real or just good publicity. This *is* show biz, after all."

"Anyone else?" you ask, trying to sound as casual as possible while furiously taking notes.

"Are you by any chance writing a murder mystery?"

"Depends on what happens next."

"What an interesting idea. You think Henry was murdered?"

"Henry?"

"Henry Baldo. That was Baldini's real name."

"Maybe."

"How exciting. Then it seems to me that the first thing you have to do is find out how he did it?"

"That's the whole point of every murder mystery, isn't it?"

"No, dear, I mean how Baldini did the Triple Escape. You'd have to understand how he got out of the boxes before you can figure out how anyone got *in*. Don't you think?"

"Do *you* know?"

"No, no. These matters are kept in strict confidence. Reputations are based on secrets in this business. I even doubt that Baldini's own assistants knew the secret of the trick. Simon might, but I doubt it."

"How would I find out then?"

"Let me see," she says, and her voice pauses and seems to hover over an invisible crystal ball. "I've got it! Another escape artist. They must have some tricks in common. But you'll have to be cagey. No one's going to give away their best tricks easily. If you come up with anything, call me back. I love mysteries! Remember, that's Madame Pollidor—Polly to you—and I'm in Room 99. Call me when you've figured it all out."

A satin curtain of silence surrounds you in the small hotel room. Before you on the night table are the telephone; a list of all the people staying at the hotel and the numbers at which they can be reached; a pencil; and a pad of paper, ripe for notes. The overhead bulb dims. The lamp on the table illuminates these innocent-looking items like a spotlight. From somewhere, the part of your brain that stores melodies perhaps, a gentle musical accompaniment begins. There is even a drumroll, if only caused by one of the hotel busboys in the hallway. Suddenly, you are on a stage of sorts. With the grace of a conjurer, you pick up the list and the pencil and begin your own private magic act . . . pulling a murderer out of a locked box.

House of Cards Hotel & Inn
Welcomes All Members of
The Society of Conjurers and Magicians
April 3—16

Member	Stage Name	Act	Room/Phone
Dierdre Peeps	Lady Dierdre	Mind Reader	03
Otto Streibnitz	The Elusive Streibnitz	Escape Artist	19
Trixon Stage	Trixon	Magician	23
Hercules Rice	(Assistant to Trixon)		18
Olivia Fray	Olivia	Card Reader	76
Henry Baldo	The Great Baldini	Escape Artist	35
Wendy Coffin	(Stage Assistant to Baldini)		35
Polly Dormus	Madame Pollidor	Clairvoyant	99
Edgar Poole	(Amateur)		08
Woodrow Beams	(Prop Assistant to Baldini)		34
Oscar Fore	(Theatre Manager for SCAM)		05
Landau	Landau the Impossible	Magician	04
Elena Melenetti	(Secretary for SCAM)		36
Eleazar Beane	Master Beane	Sleight of Hand	07
Magic Mulligan	Magic Mulligan	Magic Comedy	14
Peggy and Irv Colonski	The Nimble Colons	Jugglery	33
Noel Biggins	(Amateur)		51
Yabnalow Argyle	Count Argyle	Illusionist	44
Harman Hoodle	Dr. Hoodoo	Conjurer	12
Deanna Hoodle	(Assistant to Dr. Hoodoo)		12
Judson Wither	Judson the Great	Prestidigitator	41
Michael Millikan	Magic Millikan	Sleight of Hand	73
Vincent Melenetti	Le Grand Fantôme	Escape Artist	15
Dr. Clara Forme	(Veterinarian for SCAM)		85
Simon Penn	(Editor of SCAM newsletter)		62
Cab O'Reilly	Magical O'Reilly	Magician	37

01

"Good morning. You have reached the Hotel Services number. If you want to speak to the manager please hold on until after this message is completed. Otherwise, listen for the correct exchange for the particular service you require, then hang up and place that call separately. If you want to contact the front desk, just dial 06. If you wish to reach either Room Service or the Laundry Service, please dial . . . hello?"

"Hello?"

"Who is this?"

"Who is *this*?"

"Very funny."

"Very funny?"

"Aren't you too old for that gag?"

"What gag?"

"Repeating everything I say."

"Repeating everything?"

"There you go again. Look, in case you haven't heard, some old guy was killed this morning in the auditorium. My boss told me to keep this line open in case the police call back. Now I don't have time to play third-grade games with you. Okay?"

"I'm not playing games. I was just listening to *your* message tape."

"Message? I turned it off."

"No you didn't."

"Yes I did."

"Did not."

"Did too. And your mother's blue."

"Listen, kid," you say, trying a grown-up voice as a new ploy, "I'm trying to get in touch with *your* boss, the hotel manager. Where is he?"

"In the auditorium. I'm taking care of the office."

"How can I reach him? It's important."

"Can't. So there."

"Listen to me, you little twit. . . ."

"Bananahead."

"What?"

"Noodlebrain."

"Noodlebrain?"

"Slimesucker. No backs, no penny tax."

Click!

02

A strange clicking noise interrupts the very first ring just as you finish dialing the number. When the person at the other end begins to speak, it is clear that your call has accidentally intercepted an outgoing call he has just made.

"Juniper, my sweet, is that you?" he begins.

"Ahem!" you answer, trying to stay anonymous.

"Ah, my little wildflower. I know you can't talk now with your sisters in the same room, but I am calling to tell you how wonderful it was to have you last night. I trust you found my little Tommy Gun of sufficient caliber to hit the mark?"

"Ahem!"

"As I knew you would. Ah, my wildberry, how exquisite it was to take you that way, on the darkened stage! A dream come true. If only that idiot custodian had not come bumbling onto our love nest. But tonight! Tonight I shall ravish you with the lights on and the curtain drawn, just as we imagined! Meet me there tonight at two and we shall play out the second act of our passion play— *The Midget and the Siren*—for all the world to see."

"Ahem, ahem!"

"Yes yes, my rose petal. And until then . . . adieu!"

03

"Who's this?" barks the hoarse voice answering the phone.

"Hello?"

"Look, if you're calling to jerk me all around about old Baldini, give me a break, okay? I've had just about enough of that fat tub for one morning, dead or alive."

"Is this Dierdre Peeps," you peep.

"No, it's Princess Di. Wanna speak to Chucky? Who the hell are *you*?"

"Uh, this is Wayne E. Phipps of Phipps Insurance."

"What's the *E* for?"

"Egg," unfortunately, is the first word that comes to mind.

"Swell."

"We're in possession of an insurance policy taken out in the name of Henry Baldo—"

"Baldo? Insurance? You're out of your goddamn mind. Baldini was the cheapest son-of-a-bitch that ever took me out to dinner at Burger King. There's no way he would have paid premiums on an insurance policy. You got the wrong Baldini, Egg."

"Well, then could you tell me, Mrs. Peeps—"

"Miss. I worked hard to regain that title. Don't abuse it."

"Miss Peeps, may I get right to the point?"

"Please do. I'm not a goddamn mind reader you know."

"Did you stand to benefit from the demise of Mr. Baldo?"

"*Ha!* Benefit? Baldini's croaking is the best thing that ever happened to me! How I let that fat pig huff and puff on top of me for all those years is beyond me. I hired three different lawyers to get the old goat to cough up the alimony. You think he was good at getting out of handcuffs? You should've seen him escape responsibilities. He was a goddamn genius!"

"I see. Were you at all familiar with his Triple Water Escape?"

"You mean did I sneak in there and dump the powder in the tank? Sad to say, Egg, I didn't have the guts."

"Powder in the tank?"

"Sure, that's how he did it. I've thought of it for months, ever since I heard that the Triple uses water. All you've got to do is dump some kind of powder in the bottom of the tank that mixes with the water to make an acid or something. It's totally harmless until the water is added. Then . . . *ssst!* The fat slob would've burned in the water. Lovely thought. I'll have to write a thank-you note."

"To whom?"

"To Trixon. You know, the one with all the scarves. We used to talk about killing the Bald One over a few beers. Trixon hated him, too. Of course, anybody with half a brain did. But I didn't have the guts to actually *do* it. Does that answer your questions, Egg? I've got to go and memorize the seating plan for dinner tonight. I'm performing. The show must go on, even if your heart is breaking with joy. I really hope you find out who killed *it* so I can send flowers. Ta-*ta!*"

"Landau speaking."

"This is Dixon Trimline," you say, reading from the pencil you are using to make notes, "from the Magicians Benevolent Association. We've got some questions regarding The Great Baldini's Triple Water Escape. Are you familiar with the trick?"

"I'm familiar only with the segment that he stole from me, which I have called the Escape from a Solid Crate."

"Just as we suspected. He *did* steal part of that trick from you."

"I was foolish enough to hide my plans and designs for the crate in a safe at my office last year."

"Why was that foolish?"

"Because Henry's studio was on another floor of the same building. Once Henry is nearby, nothing is safe, not even a safe."

"You think he broke in and stole the design?"

"Of course he did."

"How do you know?"

"Because no one else *could* have broken in. He was a master lock pick."

"But isn't it possible that he came up with the same idea at the same time?"

"Precisely what my lawyers claimed and the reason I declined to file suit. In truth, however, I was able to get information from Henry's assistant, Wendy, that confirmed my suspicions."

"What kind of information?"

"Specifics of his crate design."

"Such as?"

"Why should I tell you?"

"We're putting together a case against him, a class-action suit. Should be able to recover quite a bundle from his estate. Not to mention—how shall I say—a certain degree of satisfaction for his victims?"

"Indeed. Very well then. The escape is done thusly. The crate into which one is placed is a sturdy wooden box with the planks running horizontally around the sides. All of it is solid and tight and no amount of hitting or pushing against it will disclose otherwise. But one of these horizontal panels is false. It can hinge like a door, and opens into the box."

"Why doesn't it open when people examine it?"

"This panel is held closed by two hidden spring bolts at the upper corners. The bolts stick up from this panel into the one above it, like an automatically locking door. They can't be seen from the outside."

"How are they released?"

"First of all, you must know precisely where they are. Once you do, it's a simple matter to slip a thin piece of metal into the gap and pull them back. Exactly the way one would break into a room. When you close it again from the outside, it locks shut."

"But aren't there also ropes all around the crate?"

"Ropes, chains, ribbons, tape. Whatever you'd like. They have no effect. They only prevent anything from opening *out*. But the trick panel opens *in*. You simply must leave a space to wriggle out between the restraints."

"What could go wrong?"

"Nothing."

"But something did."

"You must have a thin piece of metal or plastic with which to slip back the bolts. It's usually hidden in the crate somewhere."

"Anything else?"

"If the crate is inside another apparatus, as it apparently was for this Triple Escape, then it has to be placed correctly."

"For instance?"

"Far enough away from the inner wall of the trunk, let us say, to allow room to wriggle free from the crate. If it's too close, you can't get out. That would be Wendy's responsibility. Do you think she made an error?"

"Well, somebody sure did."

"Maybe Baldini himself. These tricks require tremendous exertion and control. Things can go wrong. Amy Curtin probably saw the whole routine. She's usually there during these rehearsals. Maybe she has an idea about it. On the other hand, maybe he just panicked."

"Why would he do that?"

"It happens."

"He doesn't sound like a man with too many fears."

"Besides hares."

"Hairs?"

"He was violently allergic to them."

"He was? Is that why he shaved his head?"

"I don't follow you."

"Was he allergic to his own hair?"

"Not hair, hares. Bunnies, rabbits, cottontails. He had a violent allergy to the little creatures. Hoodoo once gave him a rabbit's foot as a good luck charm and he almost passed out."

"From gratitude?"

"Asthma. Apparently the merest contact with rabbit hair or dander sent him gasping for breath."

"Was this a well-known fact?"

"An unknown fact. Baldini didn't like his weaknesses known."

"But Hoodoo told you?"

"We shared a certain delight in the story. Hoodoo didn't like him either—on account of some kind of bad business deal they had together. Now, if you'll excuse me . . ."

"One last question."

"Go on."

"Why aren't you listed in the directory as an escape artist if you do escapes?"

"I don't anymore. I'm getting too old to challenge idiot policemen and Boy Scouts at handcuffs and knots. I've retired to the simpler pleasures of Chinese Hoops and the Restored Cigarette. Is that all?"

05

"Is this Oscar Fore, the theatre manager for SCAM?" you ask, trying to pin him down on the first move.

"Sure is," he says, duly pinned.

"I'm calling from union headquarters, Mr. Fore. We're looking into certain allegations that—"

"What union?"

"The union. You know, *the* union," you answer, wishing you had done a little more research before the call. "Mr. Fore, were you present when Henry Baldo's props were delivered to and taken from the hotel room where they were stored yesterday?"

"Room 34. Yes."

"Why?"

"Why was I there? Because Baldini insisted on it. He wanted his props kept under close scrutiny. You might say he was slightly paranoid about it. I watched them brought into the room, then I helped his assistant, Wendy, take them down to the auditorium in the freight elevator this morning."

"Just the two of you?"

"That's right. The crate, the trunk, the hoist. They were all on wheels. We just rolled them down the hall."

"But why did he ask *you* to do it?"

"He wanted someone he could trust."

"Why you?"

"Because I'm trustworthy. Now look, what does all this have to do with UTMOST?"

"Whatmost?"

"UTMOST...the Union of Theatre Managers, Operators, and Stage Technicians. I'm all paid up."

"Not that union. I'm from MEAGRE...Metropolitan Association of Grips and Engineers. We've heard that someone may have rigged Baldini's props to fail."

"Why would anyone do that?"

"That's the second thing we want to find out."

"But no one did. I'm sure of that. They were under Baldini's own supervision right up to the front door. Then I took over and escorted them into the room. There was no time for anyone to get to them."

"Were they ever out of your sight?"

"Not until the room was locked with Baldini's own assistant inside."

"Was there anyone else around at the time?"

"Sure. Lots of people were moving in for the convention."

"Who, for example?"

"Oh, I don't remember. Let's see...Clement Sternberg was moving in on the same floor. And Laurie Delbingo came over to ask me about the size of the stage."

"Why?"

"She has a small white horse in her act. Needs a lot of room."

"Anyone else?"

"Well, that drunk Count Argyle was standing around boozing it up as usual. And so was Ollie Bemble. That's right. Ollie accidentally spilled some gin onto one of the bags. I had to ask both of them to do their drinking elsewhere."

"This Bemble spilled gin onto one of Baldini's bags?"

"Yes, a large canvas sack. Woody, Baldini's other assistant, was carrying it in. Bemble bumped into him and dumped his drink all over the bag. I knew from the smell that it was gin."

"Did you tell Baldini about that?"

"No. Neither Woody nor I wanted to bother Baldini about it. He had quite a temper, you know. It was just an accident, and besides, I knew it would dry up soon enough, so we let it go."

"What about this morning?"

"What about it?"

"You helped take the props downstairs. Did anything unusual happen then?"

"Let's see . . . Clive Adder was up doing his calisthenics, the Nutley Twins were in the hallway arguing over which of them would be sawed in half at the Ball. Oh yes, and Hyman what's-his-name, the guy who does the levitation, was frantically trying to find some thin wire. That's about it."

"And after you took the props to the stage?"

"I went back to my office down the hall."

"What happened to the props?"

"Wendy began setting them up for Baldini's practice run. Baldini was there with her. If you ask me, you people are barking up the wrong tree."

"Indeed, Mr. Fore? What do you think happened?"

"These kinds of difficult escapes involve tremendous risk. There's a great deal of exertion involved, quick reflexes, and split-second timing. This particular one was also done underwater, which made things even more dangerous. You don't need any foul play to explain the accident. The dangers are there as plain as day. Landau's told me that a million times. And he's done escapes just as difficult as the Triple Escape."

06

The phone at the front desk of the hotel rings for a very long time before a young woman picks up the receiver and answers it rather breathlessly.

"Can you believe what's going on here? I mean I can't believe what's going on here. It's just unbelievable. I mean, isn't it?"

"Front desk?"

"I mean, this guy, his name is Baldini or something, just died in the auditorium. I mean absolutely died. And Oscar wants me to stay at the front desk all morning. I mean, I've never even worked the front desk before. I don't even know how to turn the computer on and Sally is gone and Millie is filling out some kind of report. I mean, I've already done my nails and I hate this stupid intercom. It hasn't stopped ringing all morning."

"Is that so?"

"I mean, if everyone is so into this guy Baldini and everything and what happened to him, let them call up Wendy. She was his assistant. I mean, my God, she was head over heels in love with him. At least that's what she told me. So she must know what happened to him, right? Am I right?"

"Absolutely."

"I mean, at least then I can go back to what I do best, which is stamping envelopes. I don't know all this computer garbage. I mean, I'm no Alfred Einstein, for God's sake. And besides, what do I need all this grief for? I told Oscar right from the start, I said this is only a temp job until I can get into beauty school. I made it very clear. So what does he want from me? Right? Am I right?"

07

"All right, Beane, let's get down to business," you bark, after the usual opening pleasantries. "What do you know about Madame Defarge and Henry Baldo?"

"One's breathing; the other isn't."

"Cut the wisecracks, pal. We overheard a little conversation of yours yesterday. In the bathroom."

"What are you guys doing, bugging the toilets?"

"Let's just say we've got ears everywhere."

"That can get pretty messy, can't it?"

"You let us worry about that, sonny. Now why don't you save us some time and tell us about your conversation with Madame Defarge yesterday."

"Which conversation? Me and Defarge are pals. We talk a lot."

"The one where Defarge said, 'Last time it *almost* killed him. Unfortunately, he came too soon. But I'll get him tonight, Beane,'" you say, reading from your notes.

"Did she say that?"

"We've got it on tape."

"So she's a little weird. What do you expect from a six-foot-three-inch transvestite? What's that got to do with me?"

"Don't play dumb with us, Beane. Who was she talking about?"

"I'd rather not say."

"Rather talk to a grand jury?" you ask, borrowing the line from a late movie. "Spill. Who was she talking about?"

"Octopad."

"Who?"

"Clive Adder, the contortionist. She's in love with the dude, or something. They've been having this secret thing going for a few weeks. Peter's okay about it—"

"Who?"

"Peter. Madame Defarge. She's okay about it but Clive's paranoid that someone will find out. Clive thinks it'll ruin his reputation if people find out he's gay. So they've been sneaking around. They were together last night, too, but Peter made me promise not to tell anyone. For Clive's sake."

"So why did Defarge say, 'Last time it *almost* killed him. Unfortunately, he came too soon. But I'll get him—'"

"No, no. You got that all wrong. Now I know what you're talking about. She was telling me about their weirdo sex games. She's always talking about that. If Peter was really a woman, she'd be the sexiest woman I know. What she probably said was 'Last time it almost *killed* him.' Meaning some little sexual thing she was doing, some trick."

"Like?"

"I don't know and I don't want to know."

"And the other part? Where she says that he came too soon? I guess that doesn't mean he arrived too soon for the plan to succeed."

"*Came* too soon, you know, like spent himself. But what's Defarge's sex life got to do with Henry Baldo?"

"Very little, it seems."

"You think Defarge had something going with Baldo, too? Peter never said anything about that and she tells me everything. If you want the inside dope on Baldo, why don't you talk to Elena Melenetti or Harman Hoodle. They both used to work with him, I think."

08

Looking through the phone list for inspiration, you come across your own phone number. Your eyes drift to the phone on the table and without thinking, you almost pick it up as if, by the logic of a dream, it somehow made sense to give yourself a call and ask a few probing questions.

Luckily, a sound interrupts this silly reverie. The phone itself is ringing. Someone is actually calling you. You pick it up, hold the receiver to your ear, say hello. Ready for a chat. But the voice at the other end has no plans for a lengthy conversation.

"Who do," it says enigmatically, before abruptly hanging up.

10

"Cagliostro is at your service! What can I do to please you? What is your desire? All things are possible."

"I've got a few questions I'd like you to answer."

"Your wish is my commandment, your humble servant awaits, you tella big fella."

"Did you know The Great Baldini?"

"Who asks the master of the Flotational Light Bulb this question?"

"It is I...Detective Capello, Seventeenth Precinct. Master of homicide and aggravated assault."

"I see. *Polizia*. Then your questions shall be answered, your queries met, your hunches resolved. In a word, I did indeed know him. And he me!"

"How well?"

"Unwell. We occasionally bumped elbows at various bars along the circuit. I never tried to get very close to him, sensing beneath that bald dome the brain of an armadillo. In fact, there was quite a stir at our last encounter. Two weeks ago in Chicago."

"What kind of stir?"

"A tumult, a fracas, a brouhaha. We were tippling down at Mandrake's along with some fellow magicians, when there were loud shouts at the other end of the bar. I believe the words *cony, cony* were much in the air. By the time I deposited myself in the midst, there was Baldini flat on his back, being resuscitated by Hazel Wolman, who fortunately is a licensed nurse as well as conjurer."

"What happened to him?"

"This I cannot say. I had a train to catch and never found out the gruesome details of the encounter. But the presence there of Calvin Quinz suggests that he and Baldini may have had an exchange of fists."

"Why?"

"Your guess is as good as mine."

"What does *cony* mean?"

"Again, knowledge fails me. Does it perhaps refer to Coney Island, the legendary home of vaudeville magic? This, like the secrets of Stonehenge, remains shrouded in mystery. And now, my dear detective, Cagliostro must retire to his bath where await the Oils of Seven Hidden Seas and a loofa. Goodbye, farewell, and don't call me, I'll call you."

12

"Hello?" says the woman answering the phone.

"I'd like to speak to Dr. Hoodoo."

"My father is lying down. He can't come to the phone right now. He was quite shaken by the news about Mr. Baldini."

"So he knew Baldini?"

"Who is this?"

"This is Phee, my dear. From Phee, Fyphe, and Fumm. I'm a friend of your father's."

"I don't think I ever met you."

"No, you were away last time your father and I had dinner together."

"Away? But I haven't been—"

"How is he doing, Deanna? It must have been quite a blow to hear about Baldini. They were pretty close, weren't they?"

"Close? But if you're father's friend, then you must know that they didn't get along at all."

"Right! I meant close in their hatred of each other. How's he doing now?"

"Not well. Aladdin called to tell him the news a little while ago and he felt quite sick about it."

"Aladdin called, did he?"

"So did Xaviera. She wanted to warn him about repercussions. I don't know what she meant. But a lot of people called. Everyone seemed to know about the feud, even though Daddy never spoke about it much."

"You know, I was talking to a mutual friend of ours the other day and we were discussing this very matter: the feud between Baldini and your father. And for the life of me, I couldn't remember what it was all about. My mind went blank. Do you remember what it was all about?"

"But you must have heard all the rumors?"

"There are a lot of rumors about Baldini."

"Most of them true."

"Still, your father and Baldini were friends once. Weren't they?"

"I guess so. When they first started the business."

"Right. That's what I meant. When they had that business together..."

"The Correspondence School of Magical Arts."

"Of course. And what exactly caused the break between them?"

"Well, how would you feel if your own business partner robbed you blind? You'd be pretty upset, too."

"Naturally."

"And now that Baldini's dead, there'll never be any chance of Daddy getting back his bonds."

"Right, the bonds. Which bonds are those, Deanna?"

"I'm sorry. I really can't talk about all this right now. And I don't think Daddy would want me to anyway. I should go in and check on him."

"Good idea. By the way, wasn't there someone else who knew all about this sorry business with the bonds. I remember hearing that—"

"Lots of people found out about it. Daddy's a very private person, but you know how gossip spreads. Especially regarding Baldini. Mrs. Melenetti tried to keep it all quiet but she just couldn't."

"Mrs. Melenetti?"

"She was their secretary. She saw the whole thing."

14

"Hey, hey, hey! Mulligan's the name, magic's the game. I do parties, bar mitzvahs, weddings, proms. No occasion too small. For the right price, I'll even show up at breakfast and make your lox and bagel disappear. What can I do you for?"

"I'm calling about Henry Baldo," you finally manage to interject.

"Ah, old bowling-ball skull himself. Did he give you my number? Great. But I have to warn you...I'm not cheap. This isn't like the Middle Ages, you know. Magic ain't free anymore."

"This call does not concern a job, Mr. Mulligan."

"Magic, call me Magic. I had my name legally changed last year. Everyone calls me Magic, except my mom, who calls me a bum. Hey, just a joke there, pal. Don't have much of a sense of humor, do you? I sell practical jokes, too, you know. You sound like the kind of person who could use one."

"I'm calling from the Vanishing Act Funeral Home."

"Funeral? No wonder you don't think funny. But I don't know, I've never really worked a funeral before. Seems to me that if you can't pull off the Big Trick for everyone, what's a few Restored Neckties. You know what I mean?"

"We don't want to hire you. We're trying to find out your connection with the late Henry Baldo."

"Late? What time was he supposed to be there? You want me to fill in? I guess I owe him a favor after that job in the Catskills last year."

"Mr. Mulligan, aren't you aware of what's happened to The Great Baldini?"

"Don't tell me . . . his hair started growing again and he had to change his name."

"The Great Baldini died on stage this morning."

"Look, pal, if I had a nickel for every time I died on stage, I'd be writing my memoirs in Palm Springs."

"I mean died in the fatal sense."

"What? Baldini's dead? Is that what you're saying?"

"You haven't heard the commotion in the hotel all morning?"

"No, I've been locked up in the room here practicing Three Coins and a Comb. What happened to him?"

"Did you know him well?"

"I knew him like I knew my own brother . . . hardly at all. Haven't seen the bastard in seven years—my brother, that is. Baldini occasionally stole some gags from me, but then he got me a job upstate last year. That's about all."

"Do you know of anyone who may have wanted to harm Baldini?"

"Sure. Anyone who ever met him. He was a real louse. Like that whole deal with Hoodoo?"

"What deal?"

"Dunno. Some kind of flap over money. Hoodoo wasn't the only one Baldini screwed. But look, Baldini did me some favors over the years, so I can't fault the guy. You know, I once wrote a check to him in disappearing ink. Just a mistake, mind you, but you should have seen the look on his face in the bank."

"Well, thank you for your help. We'll get back in touch with you if—"

"Say listen. What about the funeral gig? I've got a great bunch of classic gags right now. People like a good laugh. How about we try out a dozen Whoopie Cushions? Nice bit, right? Please be seated? No? Too tacky? How about some Squirting Flowers . . .?"

15

"Hey, hello, what's up? Who's this? Hello? You with the papers?"

"Which papers?" you ask.

"You tell me. *Times*? *News*? I'll talk to anybody. You with the *Examiner*?"

"Sure, why not?"

"Great. I read your paper. Real rag. I guess you want to know who killed Baldini, right? Well, it wasn't me, but I know who it was. And better than that, I know *how* they did it."

"Is this Le Grand Fantôme?"

"Yea, that's me. Le Grand Fantôme, toast of Paris."

"You don't have much of an accent."

"Are you kidding? I worked years to get rid of my accent. You know how far I'd get in this business with a Brooklyn accent?"

"I take it you're not from Paris, Monsieur Fantôme."

"Call me Vinnie. Look, do you want the story or don't you? I know I'm a prime candidate to croak the Great Baloney. He stole my trunk escape for the last part of his Triple Water Hoax. But murder ain't my thing."

"Whose thing is it?"

"Look, I told two people about the secret of that trunk escape. Baldo was one and Trixon Stage was the other. We were drunk one night and I spilled the beans. Thought I could trust them. Trixon's an all right kinda guy, but see, he was real pissed off at Baldo for having an affair with his wife. I didn't know that at the time. But I figure it this way. Once they both knew the secret of the trunk escape, then they both knew how to screw it up. Trixon must've set things up to kill Baldo. It's easy to do if you know what's going on."

"Vinnie, that's exactly what our readers want to know."

"Now listen up and I'll give you the lowdown. The trunk itself is solid, made of steel with real rivets and so on. No trick panels or nothing. The lid really is attached to the rim with real padlocks. But the thing is this: the rim is a steel band running all around the top edge and it looks like it's solidly attached to the trunk. But it isn't. The rim's really attached to an inner steel sleeve that fits tight inside the trunk. Follow?"

"Not exactly."

"Like the liner of a thermos bottle. That's where I got the idea from. Imagine if you could screw on the top of a thermos bottle, then pull the top, screw threads, and inner lining out in one shot. See? That's how she works. People inspecting it can't tell nothing. But once you're inside, and the curtain's drawn, you push up against the lid and the whole top, rim, and inner sleeve—padlocks and all—slides up. You slip out, put it back in place. It slides back down by its own weight, and no one knows a thing. See?"

"Very ingenious."

"Hey, I was voted Most Likely to Escape in high school."

"And Trixon Stage?"

"Don't know. Must've gone to a different high school."

"I mean how do you think he set up the trick to kill Baldo."

"Oh, yeah. Well, the whole thing depends on being able to push up against the lid. It weighs a lot. It's hot in there, no air. And I heard that Baldo was doing it underwater, too. So it's simple. Just put a weight on top of the trunk and you can't shove it. You push and push, lose your breath, take in water, drown. That's the ticket."

"What kind of weight?"

"A hundred pounds would do it. Someone could sneak behind the curtain and put something on top of the trunk. I don't know, maybe Baldo's assistant, Wendy, went and sat on it. Could be."

"But why?"

"Maybe Stage hired her. Maybe she's got her own gripe against Baldo. Who knows? You're the reporter. Check it out. Now, did you get all that down? That's Grand Fantôme with an *e* on the end, like in French. I'll be appearing at Lou's Seafood Grille on the twenty-ninth. Hello? Hello?"

17

"Calvin Quinz?"

"Yeah yeah. What do *you* want to know? Whether I killed him, when I killed him, or only *why*?"

"Any of them will do."

"Who are you with—the papers, the cops, or the hotel?"

"All of them."

"Okay, fine. Then the answer is no."

"No what?"

"No, I didn't kill Baldini. Breaking his fat nose two weeks ago in Mandrake's was satisfying enough."

"So we've heard."

"But did you hear why I did it?"

"Why don't you tell us?"

"Because that bastard Baldo pulled a Ponzi on me."

"Was it loaded?"

"A Ponzi, not an Uzi. It's a scam. He got almost five grand before I figured out what was going on."

"Why didn't you sue him?"

"I did, but my dingbat of a lawyer couldn't convince the judge that Baldo was behind it. But I knew he was. So instead I went to Mandrake's to even the score. I knew he'd be there mouthing off about himself, and sure enough, there he was with Trixon Stage's wife. I called him a goddamn cony right to his face, then I punched him. I meant to beat him to a bloody pulp, but I stopped after I heard his nose crack."

"Why?"

"I hurt my fist. Besides, the others were holding me back."

"You say you called him a *cony*. What does that mean?"

"It's a slang term from the old sideshows. It's short for coney-catcher, which means a cheat, a swindler. That should have been Baldo's middle name. Go ask Harman Hoodle or Elena Melenetti. They know what I'm talking about."

18

The only good thing about the relentless ringing of a phone when no one is there to answer it is that it gives you time to think. The muffled bell, the rhythm of the tone, the hollow echo of the background...all conducive to brain activity.

And it is in this artificially induced state of reflection that something occurs to you. The Triple Escape had three parts. Knowing Baldini's reputation, each part was probably stolen from a different magician. So there are perhaps three different escape artists in the Society, each of whom could have sabotaged part of the trick.

The best plan is to locate all three, find out what they know, and determine which one is the murderer. Simple. Unfortunately, the hanging up of the phone disconnects these thoughts as well, and you are back where you started, staring at the list of names.

19

"Otto Streibnitz speaking. Hallo?"

"Ah, Mr. Streibnitz. I'm glad I found you in. This is Dixie Bixby of *Magicians Monthly* magazine."

"Off course you found me in. Vere should I go? Z'police half told me to shtay in z'room. Perhaps zey tink The Elusive Streibnitz hess killed Henry Baldo. Some joke, ya? *Magicians Monthly* magazine, you say?"

"Yes, we're running a special article—full feature, full color, full width, the works—on that part of the Triple Water Escape known as the escape from a sack."

"Ach! *My* sack escape. Ya, off course. Baldo shtole zet from me, he did. I vas a fool to show him my trick."

"You say you showed him how to do the escape and then he stole the trick from you?"

"I'm sure of it. Off course, no von's seen his Triple Escape, but z'moment I heard it involfed a sack, zen I knew the little pig hess shtolen my trick."

"That's exactly what we want our readers to know, Mr. Streibnitz. The truth about Henry Baldo! Now can you tell me exactly how the escape from the sack was done?"

"Giff avay z'secret? But ziss is verboten, ya? A magician does not tell his trick to z'world."

"But the world must know, Mr. Streibnitz! All those young boys and girls, our avid readers, hoping to follow in *your* footsteps and themselves, one day, be great escape artists. Don't you think they deserve the whole story?"

"Ya but . . ."

"Of course they do. Now what exactly happened in that sack once the ropes and straps were tied? Did he have some sort of untying device with him?"

"Ha. Zet's vat everyone tinks. Z'heavy leather straps, buckles, und ropes . . . ze more z'better. But it's all irrelevant, only meant to mislead z'audience. You don't go out true dat vay, you go out true z'bottom hem."

"Hem?"

"Ya, ze hem dat holds ze sack closed. See, mitt all dese straps and ropes and so on, no one tinks of ze hem on ze bottom. No von looks much at it. Every sack has von, mitt elaborate stitching—how do you say?—heavy duty. But on ziss sack, it's made special. Ze fancy stitching don't go all the vay true. Just for show, on ze outside. Vot really holds ze hem closed is a simple single stitch of nylon thread. Ze one who inspects the sack maybe pulls at ze hem to see that it's strong, and it is. But inside, under the cover of the box or a curtain, you take out a small razor blade und cut true the nylon thread. Very easy, ten seconds at ze most. Zen, when you're out of ze sack, you stitch it back up with another line of thread on a needle you've concealed in ze mouth, perhaps, or in your shoe. Ze ones who inspect the sack in the end see only zat it's still intact. Nobody checks it too carefully anyvay. Everyone much too busy mitt ze leather straps and buckles."

"So if Baldo used this method for the trick . . ."

"Off course he used it! It's foolproof, even for such a fool."

"Then he simply had to cut through a single line of thread, get out of the sack, and sew it back up. How long would all that take?"

"For a master like myself . . . thirty seconds. For a schvein like Baldo . . . one minute."

"It doesn't sound very difficult to do."

"Exertion, dat's the difficult part. Ze sack is tight, heavy canvas. Zere's no air. You must find ze hem, position it, cut it, sew it again. It takes dexterity. Good breath. Particularly if you're hanging upside down over Lake Michigan like I vas last vinter."

"Or underwater. Tell me, Mr. Streibnitz, suppose someone wanted to undermine the trick, foil it. What's the best way to do that?"

"I don't follow you."

"Suppose someone wanted to make sure you *wouldn't* get out of the sack."

"Thread zat can't be cut. Metal vire perhaps instead of nylon. Or glue it closed."

"But then you could still cut out through the side."

"Ya. Zen maybe dull z'razor blade. Mitt a dull blade you couldn't cut true ze canvas. Off course, a good assistant vould check all dese tings out very carefully. Zat vas Vendy's job."

"Vendy? You mean Wendy?"

"Ya, Baldini's assistant. But vhy should anyvone vant to do such a ting?"

"That's great, Mr. Streibnitz, you've been a tremendous help. All our budding magicians will be thrilled to hear all this, we'll be sure to send you a free copy of the article. Keep that subscription up to date. *Auf Wiedersehen.*"

"Vot subscription?"

20

"Luther Rebob here, your East Coast rep for Mongo Magic and World O'Magic, with the bestest and mostest in magical and mystical supplies. I've got specials running all month on colored scarves, foam balls, and flash pots. Tell me the trick and you can have your pick. Whadaya need?"

"Information."

"There's an odd request. But nothing's too weird for Luther Rebob, your personal magic supply house. Let me look in Mongo Magic's unique 230 page catalogue, available for free with a minimum purchase of twenty-five dollars, and see what I can find."

"Forget the catalogue, Rebob. I'm the bookkeeper for Mongo Magic. I need some information about the items you've sold in the last few days."

"I sent in all the purchase orders on Thursday."

"Right. Those are fine. But I need to find out about any supplies you may have sold during the convention."

"It only started yesterday. Give me a chance."

"So you haven't sold any yet?"

"Sure I have. But no bulk. It's mostly little things to

get ready for the ball. The last day of the convention is the big sales day."

"Exactly what little things have you sold so far? And to whom?"

"Well let's see ... Trixon Stage bought three colored scarves for $9.99. That's the little ones, not the midis. Cab O'Reilly came to look at stage razors but he didn't take one. I sold him some flash pot powder instead. The pint. Madame Defarge—she's that weirdo transvestite—bought a jar of Snake Oil lubricant. Hyman Rosen wanted some stage wire but I didn't have any. You should probably stock some of that."

"Is that all?"

"That's it. Oh, one of the Birks came in and bought my last Dragon's Breath flame thrower. Have supply send another few over here. I usually sell four or five of them during the open house."

"Flame thrower?"

"It's a popular item. In a pinch, it's a good way to divert the audience's attention. Which reminds me, I never got my commission rebate for last month."

"Take it up with sales."

"That'll take months. You do the books. Can't you look into it? I live for those commissions. You think I enjoy sitting in these lousy hotel rooms selling Floating Flowers and Wonder Balls to these morons? If I have to look at another Vanishing Pencil, I'm going to puke. The only thing that makes it bearable is the damn commission check. What do you say? Will you look into it?"

"Sorry, not my department. Thanks for your help. Goodbye."

"You people really burn me. You sit there all day at a nice cozy desk while I'm out here busting my ass to sell your lousy products, half of which don't even work. Why don't you take a nice five-in-one Miracle Wand—the jumbo size—and shove it up your ass!"

21

"Yuh?"

"I'd like to speak to the custodian."

"That's me. Willy."

"Were you there this morning when the accident happened?"

"Which one?"

"Baldini."

"Who?"

"The guy who drowned."

"Oh, him. Well I was outside in the hallway fixin' a light. So I heard this gal screamin' her head off and I come in and seen her trying to yank some big guy out of a tub of water on stage."

"What did you do?"

"Helped her yank. This guy was big. We got him out, laid him down on the stage, and then Mr. Fore came along and started pumpin'."

"Pumping what?"

"You know, like in the movies. Pumpin' the water out. One, two, push. One, two, push. Like that. Didn't do no good, though."

"Then what?"

"Mr. Fore tells me to go ring number 91 and say we got a medical emergency. So some guy comes down and starts pumpin', too. Still no good. Then pretty soon it's the paramedics and the cops and whatnot. They didn't need me no more, so I went back to fix the light."

"Did you notice anyone around the stage before Baldini started doing the trick?"

"Who?"

"Baldini. The guy who drowned."

"Nah. Me, Amy, Mr. Fore. But we all left the room before the guy started. He didn't want no one around. Then, like I says, next thing I know this gal is screamin' her head off and yanking the guy out of a tub of water."

"Thanks for your help."

"These here magicians are strange. I mean last night I catch one of them sneakin' around the stage in the friggin' dark. 'Stage's closed; what're you doing?' I says to him. 'Just checking things out,' he says. And he's buttonin' up his pants like he just took a leak or somethin'."

"Who was it?"

"Who?"

"The guy on the stage."

"You said his name was Blini or somethin'."

"Not him, the guy buttoning up his pants."

"Dunno. Short little guy, though. I mean real short. Like a midget."

23

"I'd like to speak to Trixon Stage, please," you say, trying to ooze familiarity.

"I'm sorry, Mr. Stage cannot come to phone at the moment. He's asleep. He's asked me to take all his calls."

"And you are . . .?"

"His assistant Herc."

"Ah, yes, Hercules," you say, locating the name on your list. "My name is Reeves. I'm from *Who's Who in American Magic*. We're working on the bios for our next edition and I'm following up on a few of the biggies: Trixon Stage, Baldini, Dr. Hoodoo. Thought I could get some information from Stage about his life and career. Whadaya say?"

"I'm sure Mr. Stage would love to assist you, but this isn't a good time. He isn't feeling very well. He has a qualm upon the stomach. Next week perhaps?"

"No good, Herc. We go to press tomorrow. Hey, maybe you can fill me in."

"I don't think—"

"Great. Just a few details of the old career. No big

deal. Like for example, how long has Stage been in the biz?"

"His entire life. His mother and father were both—"

"Great. I knew you could help. Next, what's the old boy's connection with Henry Baldo?"

"Baldo worked for Mr. Stage a few years ago. He was the warm-up."

"Didn't get that, Herc. Who warmed who up?"

"Baldini warmed up the audience before Mr. Stage went out to do his act. That was about ten years ago."

"And then?"

"And then Baldini went out on his own. Now I think that's about all I can—"

"How'd they get along, Stage and The Great Baldini? Pals?"

"He wasn't Great in those days, just Baldini. I suppose they got along all right."

"Then why'd they split up?"

"There were conflicts."

"Like what?"

"Private disagreements."

"Such as?"

"What does this have to do with—"

"Herc, old boy! You want to set the record straight, don't you? We've got tons of stuff from Baldini's side. Now let's get your boss's view of it."

"I doubt that Mr. Stage would want these matters—"

"Okay, you want it off the record? You got it. Now, what kinds of disagreements? Over routines?"

"No, wives."

"Come again?"

"Baldini made a play for Mr. Stage's wife. In fact, it was the cause of their divorce."

"You mean she went off with Baldini?"

"Yes. It was quite a blow to Mr. Stage."

"Really loved the old gal?"

"That too. But do you realize how difficult it is to find someone to do the Fiery Cage of Death? It takes months of training in timing and contortion. It practically ruined his act for an entire season."

"And what about Baldini and the wife?"

"They split up a few months later. But not before she told Baldini all the secrets of the Fiery Cage trick. The collapsing cage, the mirror, everything. Three months later it was all in Baldini's act. Mr. Stage was devastated by the whole thing. He has a very weak stomach. We had to go to Europe to help him recover."

"So I guess he wasn't too choked up when he heard about Baldini's untimely death this morning."

"*Au contraire.* Mr. Stage is not a man to let past injustices color his emotions. In fact, he was quite—as you say—choked up."

"You know, Herc, there are rumors floating around that Baldini might have been murdered."

"Perish the thought!"

"Naturally, Stage's name has come up in connection with this."

"What? Mr. Stage involved in some way with a... murder? That's the silliest thing I've ever heard. Mr. Stage could not harm a flea. Absurd."

"Let's face it, Baldini wasn't exactly his first choice for a dinner party."

"Nonsense. Even after all Baldini did, Mr. Stage still refused to hold a grudge. That's the kind of man he is. A wonderful, caring man. A charming man. A man of infinite compassion."

"Gimme a break here, Herc, will ya? This is *Who's Who,* not *Family Circle.*"

"Besides, Baldini stole tricks from everyone. It was common knowledge. Ask the other escapists. I've heard he built his entire Triple Escape on their hard work. Now if you'll excuse me, I believe I have spent more than enough time in this idle chitchat."

"Okay, Herc, you've been a real pal. Now listen, if Stage wakes up and wants to talk to me, if anything comes to mind that he thinks I should know about him or Baldini, just tell him I can be reached at number 08. That's the room I'm staying in. Got it? *Ciao* for now."

25

"Greetings from Mambo Jumbo, the Prince of Nubia. Who is calling the Master of the Black Arts?"

"This is Perkins from *Wild Kingdom*, prince of the TV show."

"Ah, the media. Mambo loves television. Did you know that his appearance on *Star Search* led to a commercial for a major soft drink?"

"Which one?"

"The Prince of the Nile is not at liberty to say until the final contracts are approved. But be confident that Mambo's press agent will put you on the mailing list for all future news releases. Now, what is it you wish to know?"

"We wish to know if you use any hare in your act."

"Ah, I see. And why is Magic Jumbo's use of any hair of interest to the television audience?"

"I'm sure they're interested in any details about the great Mambo Jumbo."

"Of course, of course. Yes, it is true, the Lord of Lower Zambia does use a series of shrunken heads during a segment of the show entitled 'The Sacrifice to Fierce Mombatu.' Each of these has a full head of hair, not to mention eyelashes and, in three cases, beards."

"Not that kind of hair, Prince. The hoppity kind."

"Hoppity? King Voodoo seems to be missing the point."

"I'm talking about a rabbit."

"As in bunny rabbit?"

"The very same."

"Ah, yes. Mambo did once use a bunny rabbit in the Devil Dance routine but, sadly, the small creature got sick with a rabbit fever and had to eventually be discarded in favor of a mamba."

"A what?"

"A snake. A marvelous snake who has now become Mambo's trademark."

"No more rabbit?"

"Best to leave bunny rabbits to the others. After all, Mambo Samba looks rather foolish with a tiny little rabbit in his massive hands. It is for Duke Melenetti, with the small pale hands of a cardsharp, to handle a rabbit. For the great Mambo, Lord of Voodoo, however, nothing less than the ten-foot poisonous mamba of the Congo will suffice."

26

"You're just the person I want to talk to," Preston Change says after you've identified yourself as one of his biggest fans. "I've got a new trick I'm going to perform tonight. Tell me what you think. I ride out on stage dressed in full armor on top of a horse. My attendants, all dressed in black leotards, pull a curtain around me and the nag and—*boom!*—when the curtain's pulled back I'm gone from the horse, nowhere to be seen. Sound good?"

"Sounds fine. Mr. Change, did you know Henry Baldo?"

"No. I mean, does it matter to you that the horse doesn't disappear, too? Does that make me look like an amateur?"

"Not at all. You *do* know that Henry Baldo was killed this morning while rehearsing?"

"I heard. Now you have to remember, there's music and pageantry going on the whole time and you can hear the armor rattling. So it's a lot more impressive than I'm making it sound over the phone."

"I'm sure it is. Have you heard the rumors that foul play might be involved?"

"Of course. Maybe I should also carry a lance. That'll give the whole scene more sense of danger. I wonder if Drew Scriver's busy this morning? Think a lance is a good idea? Or maybe a shield?"

"Lance. Any idea who might have wanted to kill Baldini?"

"What makes you think that?"

"I'm a fool for a good lance."

"About Baldini. What makes you think someone killed him?"

"An imposing list of suspects."

"So I've heard. Like Trixon Stage, Dierdre Peeps, Harman Hoodle. You may be right. Besides, a magician would make a good murderer."

"Why?"

"Because the perfect murder and the perfect magic trick are based on the same principle."

"Which is?"

"Misdirection. A pile of fictions that hide the actual fact. Take my armor trick, for example. Everything that happens on stage is just meant to misdirect the audience's attention. The commotion of the attendants, the movements of the horse. Even the clanging of the metal is just loud sound effects. I sit on the horse as though the suit of armor weighs a ton. But it's misdirection, just meant to hide a simple fact."

"Namely?"

"That the whole suit of armor is made of paper. It's just metallic paper over a paper framework. When the curtain's drawn I just rip it off, roll it up into a big wad, and stuff it under the saddle."

"No kidding? But how do *you* disappear?"

"More misdirection. I'm wearing leotards underneath, just like the others. When my attendants pull back the curtain I just join them. The audience has been so busy watching the armor and the pageant, they never bothered to count the number of attendants. That's the trick. I'll bet that if someone killed Baldini, they *didn't* do it by rigging his props. No misdirection. See what I mean? Now, what about a lance *and* a shield?"

28

"What is going on here, Olivia? Were we disconnected? I mean, I am not a bit surprised considering that Baldinimania has taken over the entire hotel. My phone has not stopped ringing since early this morning with people gossiping and accusing and absolutely going out of their minds over that fat old man. I mean I am truly sorry about him and all that, but this has simply been one of the worst days of my life—between Olive, who insists that she can't go on tonight because she has her period, and Juniper, who thinks *she's* in love with that horrible little midget that I've absolutely forbidden her to see. I mean I *am* their older sister but there are limits to my patience for all this and then, in the middle of everything, that Dragon's Breath flame thrower that I bought from Luther Rebob to add a little pizzazz to the Urn trick—well, it's an absolute dud. It's going to look about as impressive onstage as a Bic lighter. I mean, what am I going to do? I've invited my mother to see the show tonight and *she* won't talk to Olive because of the Mother's Day thing and Juniper won't talk to Mother's new boyfriend and, on top of everything else, I ate so much on that idiotic cruise last month that I absolutely cannot close my sequined toga. I'm going to look like a gift-wrapped sausage on stage. I mean, my question is: is absolutely *anything* going right?"

32

"General Magic's the name, general magic's the game. Floating dice, disappearing bottles, scarves from an empty tube—you name it. Guaranteed to preoccupy the mind of even the most jaded party guests, not to mention cranky five-year-olds. Reasonable rates. How may I serve you?"

"You can tell us a bit about The Great Baldini."

"Ah, that sad and poignant moment in magical history. Brief, too brief is that earthly jaunt, my friend. Have you ever seen me resurrect a dead parrot?"

"Mr. Sternberg, let me get to the point. We at the Great Baldini Fan Club and Choir are interested in a different type of trick. The one where someone is able to cause the death of our hero and make it look like an accident."

"So the game's afoot, eh? You think someone did old Baldo in? A dastardly deed, indeed, my friend. And have you assembled a snare of suspects to enweb this devil?"

"What?"

"In a word . . . whodunit?"

"That's exactly what we're hoping you'll be able to help us find out."

"So General Magic's renown for amazing cerebration hath preceded him. And who, may I ask, among my coterie directed you thus?"

"Huh?"

"Who gave out with my number, O ye of the mundane ear."

"You were seen in the hallway when Baldini's props were being moved into Room 34."

"Oh. So what's that got to do with the price of wax?"

"We're following up on a lead that someone may have rigged the props. We wondered if you noticed anything."

"Right there, in full view and daylight? Unlikely, my friend. Most unlikely. I see someone sneaking into the room late at night, under cover of foul darkness, and messing with the locks."

"Which locks?"

"Any locks. It's easy to jam locks. You just break off a piece of metal inside. Baldini was preparing for his Triple Escape, yes?"

"Yes."

"So there must have been locks. Handcuffs? Padlocks?"

"But there was someone guarding them all night long."

"Locks come cheap, my friend, but greed is cheaper."

"You mean someone could have bribed his assistant?"

"You surprise me. Your mind is more subtle than the rusty post I first imagined."

"Any idea who would do such a thing?"

"Read me your list and I shall signal probabilities with an affirmative grunt."

"You already have the list of suspects. It's the list of SCAM members they gave out for the convention."

"Ah so. Then you are at the dim beginning of this convolution. Baldini, I trust your first feeble peeks have ascertained, was a brute and a boor. He had no end of enemies. But there is one name on this list that seems to shimmer with the heat of guilt."

"Yes?"

"Clive Adder."

"Why?"

"That, youthful sleuth, is for you to find out and me to know. Let's just say Adder was profoundly immersed in what one might call a blind rage concerning the dearly departed. And the fact that he is also a contortionist, one able to pretzelize his very being out of existence, leads one to note a certain handy talent."

"You mean he might have gotten into Room 34 in secret?"

"The ability of intelligences of your caliber to discern the obvious from related facts is an unceasing source of entertainment. In a word . . . yup."

"Can I ask you one last question?"

"Be brief. This conversation has begun to wear down my stamina."

"I've always wondered how the Scarves from an Empty Tube trick is done."

"Wonder is good for the soul."

"Even a hint?"

"Let us make a deal, you and I. I shall agree to explain to you the arcane logic of the Empty Tube trick if you, for your part, agree to buzz off and ne'er darken my phone again with your juvenile prattle."

"I'm not sure what you just said but I agree to it."

"Fine. The tube in question is one foot and a half long. It is held up to the audience, who can clearly see through it all the way to my beneficent countenance at the far end. I place the tube down on the table, resting on the end that faced the audience, and begin pulling scarves from it like there was no tomorrow. Are you still alert?"

"Yes."

"The tube is in two parts, an outer cylinder and an

inner sleeve. The two pieces fit together perfectly at the end I show to the audience. But at the other end, which I hold away from the crowd, the inner sleeve slowly decreases in diameter. Thus, an empty space or compartment is formed between the inner and outer parts and this is where the scarves are hidden. From the viewpoint of the mob, the narrowing seems a result merely of the laws of perspective. It is never noticed."

"Gee."

"Well stated, indeed. I trust that satisfies your febrile curiosity? And now, I fear that nothing less than a cold shower will cure me of your insidious probings. Good-bye."

33

"What is it now, you sap?"

"Pardon me?" you say, thinking you've misunderstood the question.

"No way, José. You want a pardon, go ask the governor for one. I've had it with you, butterfingers. Some juggling act we've got. My father was right about you. You couldn't catch a cold if it was shoved up your nose."

"Is this Peggy Colonski?"

"Wait a minute, who is this? Irv?"

"No, it isn't Irv."

"Oh Christ. I'm sorry. You got me right in the middle of a fight with my husband. I thought it was him calling to apologize. He went down to the bar to try to juggle a few drinks. That's about all he can handle, too. What a clod! Can you believe I left my mom and dad to hook up with this guy? Said he was a juggler. You know how many glasses he's broken in the last week?"

"Eyeglasses?"

"No, wineglasses. That's what we've been working on. One bottle, six glasses. In the last move, I toss them to him one by one and he fills them. But the guy's got hands like Teflon. You know what I mean?"

"Mrs. Colonski, we've heard a report that there was a loud crash in your room late last night. Would you mind telling me—"

"See what I mean? Case in point. I told that jerk everyone would hear it. It's just not good for a juggler's rep to hear crashes all the time. That's what we've got in common with pilots."

"What?"

"You know, pilots and jugglers both hate crashes. We were up late practicing so we could perform it at the Ball. The wineglass trick, that is. Okay. We go through the usual pattern—three and three—no big deal. Then I toss him two glasses, then the bottle and—*boom!*—he conks himself with the bottle, goes flying into the table, and slams into the wall. Broke four new glasses in one move. What a sap! Plus, he's whimpering 'cause he cut his hand and can't perform and I'm screaming 'cause he couldn't perform even if he had a third hand. And now the whole hotel knows it! Now take my father...there was a juggler. Like my mom used to say, he never dropped anything but his pants. You know what I mean?"

34

"Hello, Mr. Beams?"

"Yes?"

"You were Henry Baldo's prop assistant, weren't you?"

"Yes."

"I'm from Able Prop Assurers Limited. I'd like to ask you a few questions."

"Okay."

"We understand that Baldini had a great deal of security around his props. Is that true?"

"Yes."

"What was your job exactly, Mr. Beams?"

"Props."

"I know that, Mr. Beams. But what did you do to the props?"

"Watched 'em."

"Why?"

"Protection."

"From what?"

"Tampering."

"Don't you ever answer a question with more than one word?"

"Sure."

"All right, Beams, the jig is up," you say, trying to shake a whole sentence from him. "We've got a policy out on those props and there are going to be plenty of lawsuits flying in the next few days. Give me one good reason why I shouldn't turn your name over to the police."

"Me?"

"Forget the cover-up, sonny. We know all about you. You hated Baldo. You wanted to do him in, so you rigged one of the props to fail on cue. What was it, son, the crate? The trunk?"

"I didn't rig anything."

"Ah, four words. Now we're getting somewhere. Spill the beans, Beams. What did you do last night?"

"Slept."

"Alone?"

"No."

"Ah! A little nooky, eh, Beams? I smell a conspiracy. Who'd you sleep with?"

"The props. That was my job."

"Come again?"

"Henry rented the room next to his to store the props for the trick: the sack, the crate, the trunk, the curtain, all of it."

"Doesn't the hotel have a storage room?"

"He didn't trust it. He always kept his props in a separate room. They were locked in the room yesterday and I was stationed inside. At night, I slept on a cot there. This morning I helped Oscar and Wendy—she's the stage assistant—take them down to the auditorium."

"No hanky-panky, is that what you're saying?"

"Of course not. I'd put myself out of a job. I only started working for him a month ago. I'm still on probation. All I did was make sure that nobody got near the props. And nobody did. And I didn't hate Henry. I just didn't like him much."

The voice, you can now tell having heard more of it, is not that of a crafty criminal at all. It belongs to a shy young man. And you alter your approach to fit the insight.

"Did you notice anything unusual while the props were in that room?"

"Not exactly."

"What, exactly, did you notice?"

"Well, there was a knock on the door at about 2 A.M. I wasn't supposed to open the door but it sounded like someone fell down outside. It turned out to be Count Argyle, drunk. His room was just above the one I was in. I guess he was confused, as usual, so I just closed the door and went back to sleep."

"Is that it?"

"There was a loud crash at about three in the morning. Sounded like it came from Room 33, next door to the room I was in."

"I thought you said Baldo was next door."

"He was in 35. I'm in 34, where the props were. The sound came from 33. I went back to sleep and didn't wake up again until the rabbit."

"Rabbit?"

"Yes, one of the rabbits must have escaped and found its way into the prop room."

"How?"

"Vent, I guess. There's an air vent near the floor in the room and the cover was off."

"Baldini's rabbit?"

"No, he didn't use any. But a lot of the others do. There are lots of animals at the convention: rabbits, dogs, pigeons. That's why they have a vet in the Society."

"What did you do with it?"

"Nothing. I couldn't find it when we moved the props out. Maybe it went out the same way it came in."

"Did you tell Baldo about any of this?"

"No, I didn't see him. Only Oscar and Wendy."

"Who is Oscar?"

"He's the theatre manager. He was the one who came up with Wendy to bring the props down to the auditorium. Henry met them downstairs."

"All right, Beams. You've turned out to have a few sentences in you after all. Sorry about that rough stuff before, but we've got to get to the bottom of this right away. Don't leave your room, though. We might have more questions later."

"Okay."

35

"Hello?" says a frail voice at the other end of the line.

"Is this Wendy Coffin?" you say, trying to sound trustworthy.

"Yes, it is. Who is this?"

"I'm calling from the county sheriff's office. The name is...Masterson. We're looking into the tragic death of—"

But your carefully rehearsed part is interrupted by a sad moan that soon blossoms into uncontrollable wailing. It takes quite a long time before the young woman has calmed herself enough to return to the conversation, a point signaled by a loud honk into a handkerchief.

"I'm sorry, but you see, I'm still so upset about the accident. Oh God, seeing him lying there like that, just floating in the water like a little frog. I just can't get that image out of my mind."

"Floating in the water? Outside of the wooden crate? Is that what you mean?"

"Yes. It was horrible."

"Then he must have successfully escaped from the first two parts of the trick, the canvas sack and the wooden crate."

"Floating just like a little frog."

"So something must have gone wrong with the trunk."

"Oh no. It looked exactly the way I left it before I closed the curtain around it."

"Were there handcuffs as well?"

"He didn't use them for the practice."

"Wasn't it your job to check everything over before he began the trick?"

"Oh yes, and I did, just as I was supposed to do."

"What did you do, exactly?"

"Sweetpea—I mean Mr. Baldo—told me to look over the canvas sack, especially at the stitching along the bottom hem, and to tug at it to make sure it was tight. It was."

"What else?"

"Then I had to check the wooden crate to make sure all the planks were solid and firm, and they were. And finally, I had to make sure there was nothing obstructing the trunk once it was closed. There couldn't be anything on top of it or blocking it. And there wasn't."

"Nothing unusual."

"Nothing at all."

"Do you know how the escapes were done, Miss Coffin?"

"Oh no. Sweetpea . . . Mr. Baldo . . . hadn't told me that yet. He wanted me to just concentrate on what I was doing. He was going to tell me afterward. But then . . . there never was an afterwards . . . because . . . there he was, floating in the water . . . just like a little frog."

You wait for a few more sobs to subside before continuing.

"Just a few more questions, Miss Coffin. What did you do this morning to set up the rehearsal?"

"I went to the prop room with Oscar Fore, the manager, and we wheeled everything down to the auditorium. Sweet—Mr. Baldo met us there and we moved everything into place. Then he cleared the auditorium of everyone except me and we began the rehearsal."

"Does anyone else ever have access to the props?"

"If a fitting on the trunk needs adjusting or something like that, there's a technician in the Society that does it. But that wasn't necessary for these props because they were new."

"Who made these props?"

"Mr. Baldo had different people work on parts of them so no one person knew the whole trick."

"Anyone else handle them?"

"Well, there's Woody. Woody is the prop boy. He had been guarding those props with his life all night long."

"And that's all?"

"Yes. Oh God, I hope I didn't make a mistake. You don't think I accidentally . . . ?"

"And what happened when the trick was over?"

"I counted to twenty, pulled back the curtain, and then started to undo everything. Once I took the lid off the trunk and saw him there I must have started screaming. Then someone came and tried to help me pull him out of the tank and then there was a doctor trying to revive him. It was so horrible. My poor old Sweetpea floating in the water just like a little—"

"Yes, frog. So you've said. Did you notice anything else unusual or unexpected this morning?"

"Just the mess."

"What mess?"

"Everything was supposed to be intact when I opened it all up. That's the whole idea of the trick. It's supposed to look like he vanished from inside. The sack was supposed to be closed inside the sealed crate. But that wasn't the way it was."

"No?"

"No, it was a mess. His leg was stuck in an open panel of the crate and the sack was wrapped around his foot. His arms were scraped."

"It sounds like the trick wasn't exactly going according to plan. Like he was struggling desperately to get out...."

But the picture you are painting is already too clear in Wendy Coffin's mind, and her end of the conversation collapses again into pitiable bawls.

36

"Are you a cop?" asks a hoarse-voiced woman.

"That depends," you say, caught off guard by her query.

"On what?"

"On how much you like cops."

"Hate'm. If you're calling about Baldini, I'll only talk to reporters."

"Well, it just so happens that I'm Brown from the *Sun*."

"Too bad. Try using some number-fifteen lotion next time."

"The *Sun-Times*. The newspaper."

"Finally! What took you people so long? I've been waiting all morning to tell the media about this story."

"Wait no more. My pencil is sharp, my pad blank. So what's the scoop?"

"How do I know you're not really a cop?"

"Look, if I told you I was a cop, you'd know I was really just a reporter trying to get the story, right? Well, I didn't, so that proves I'm not. Now shoot, I've got a deadline. You knew Baldini?"

"I worked for him. Him and Harman Hoodle. They

started this business together a few years ago. A correspondence school for teaching magic. It was just the four of us. Harman, Baldo, me, and Ollie Bemble. But Ollie and me ... well, we were really working for Harman. That louse Baldini didn't do a thing except try to hop in the sack with all the temps."

There is a pause while she takes a long drag on a cigarette, and another as she blows the smoke into the receiver. The sound alone is enough to make you cough.

"Well, the business never really got off the ground because of this thing that happened between them. You getting all this down, Brown?"

"In black and white. Go on."

"Harman had this inheritance he was using to finance the school. It was a portfolio of bonds, worth about a hundred and fifty grand. It was all the money he had. They were bearer bonds, anybody could cash them in. He kept them in a safe in his office, a real elaborate safe with three different locks and a timer and whatnot. Impossible to break into. Unless you happen to be an expert lock pick. Well, guess what?"

"One day Harman came into the office to find that the bonds were gone."

"You got it. The cops concluded that a burglar had broken in and stolen them."

"Cops are dopes."

"Brown, I like your style."

"But you, Harman, and Bemble thought Baldini did it."

"It had to be. All escapists are expert lock picks. He denied it, of course, and there was no way to prove it. But if you know Baldini, you know it's got to be true. The guy wasn't exactly Father Teresa. But what could we do? There was no proof. So we just folded the business and we all went our separate ways. And Baldini, with the luck of the fat and ugly, got away with it."

"And Harman?"

"All his money was gone. What can I say? He's been making out all right lately, but he's a very private man. Who knows what he thought about the whole thing."

"That's quite a little story."

"You just make sure people get to read it. I've been listening to rumors about it for years. Everyone's got a story to tell about Baldini. Even that putz Keifer Holbein was chewing my ear about some garbage. But what he did to Harman, that was a real crime. And now that Baldini's finally managed to do himself in, I want people to know what really happened. It would be a pity if that louse got an SRO crowd at his wake."

37

"Cab O'Reilly please."

"Speaking."

"This is Inspector Pector of the sheriff's office. I'm conducting an investigation into the death of Henry Baldo this morning."

"So?"

"So, I was wondering if you had any information about him you would like to tell us about."

"No."

"You did know Baldini, didn't you?"

"Sure. Everyone knew the Bald One."

"But you knew him a little better than most."

"Did I?"

"Didn't you?"

"No."

"All right, O'Reilly, let's stop pussyfooting around. You're at the top of my list of suspects. Fess up. Make it easier for yourself. Baldo ran off with your wife, didn't he? You hated his guts, tried to sabotage the Triple Escape, made it look like an accident. We know what you did and how you did it. So come clean. Maybe we could work out a deal."

"What wife?"

"Connie O'Reilly?"

"Oh, her. So she ran off with Baldini? Who cares?"

"You. Enough to kill your rival in a jealous rage."

"Bah! Wives come and go. I've had six of them. I never hold a grudge. Once they leave, I give them a pat on the can, a hundred bucks, and wish them luck."

"Cut the tough-guy ruse, O'Reilly. If you're so blasé about losing her, then why were you down at Drew Scriver's workshop discussing ways of sabotaging Baldini's Triple Escape?"

"Drew told you that?"

"She sure did. Do you deny it?"

"She can be a real lamebrain sometimes."

"Were you asking her about the sack escape or not?"

"Was. But it had nothing to do with Connie. Hell, I haven't thought of her in six years, until you just mentioned it. I *was* asking Drew about the sack routine, though. She had some good ideas, too."

"About how to kill Baldini!"

"About how to take some of the wind out of his bag. See, nobody could stand Baldini except a few of those ditzy broads who were impressed by his load of bull. The rest of us thought he was a jerk. So I had this bet with Seigel that you could screw up the trick and make Baldini look bad. It turns out there's an easy way to do it, too. You just slip his assistant a phony razor blade. Then he can't cut his way out of the sack and he's stuck."

"And therefore he'd drown once the sack was lowered into the water."

"Exactly. I won the bet."

"You may have won more than that."

"Yeah? Like what?"

"Like thirty to life."

"I didn't actually do it. It was just a mind game. All I had to do was prove to Seigel that it was possible. He admitted it and forked over the two bucks. End of story."

"You expect me to believe that you went through all this just to win a two-dollar bet, and didn't actually try to do it?"

"I didn't do it. Ask Wendy, his assistant. She was the one who handed him the razor blade."

"Maybe she'd lie to protect you."

"Forget it. She was in love with the big ape. Anyway, you're the police, right? So you must have picked up the razor as evidence. If it's a fake, I certainly didn't plant it. Well, is it?"

"We'll have to check into that."

"Besides, all the props were kept under lock and key by Woody. It would have been impossible to get in there and switch razor blades without him knowing about it."

"Who?"

"Baldini's prop assistant. He guarded all Baldini's stuff. Don't tell me you didn't interview him yet?"

"We'll be getting back to you shortly, O'Reilly. Don't leave the room until you hear from us."

"Sheesh! You guys get dumber all the time."

38

"Mr. Boxliner, I'm from the DA," you say, hoping to unsteady your quarry with an early jab.

"Good heavens. Is this about Baldini?"

"So, you already know about it. But how much do you know? That's the question."

"Well, I only know what I've heard on the phone this morning. He died while trying to escape from a trunk or something."

"That's right, a sack, a crate, and a trunk. We need info, mister, and we need it fast. How he did it, who did it to him, and why. What can you tell us?"

"What did you say your name was?"

"Um . . . Mason. DA's office. How exactly did Baldini *do* the Triple Escape?"

"That's odd. My brother works at the district attorney's office. I'll ask him if he knows you. Ummason, that's the name?"

"Just Mason, no um," you explain. Then, quickly changing your tack: "Not that DA. I'm from Deluders Anonymous. Baldini was a member. Poor man, suffered from a compulsive need to fool people. We think someone—the brunt of one of his little tricks perhaps—was trying to get back at him. Maybe went a bit too far."

"You think he was killed on purpose, too?"

"Too? Do you?"

"Not me."

"Who?"

"Olivia Fray. You know, the card reader. She told me this morning that she thought Baldini was murdered by Judson Wither because Baldini was having an affair with Judson's wife."

"How?"

"The usual way, I guess."

"What way is that?"

"The missionary position?"

"No, no. I mean how do you think Judson killed Baldini?"

"I have no idea."

"You must have some idea. Don't all escapists have some tricks in common?"

"I suppose they do."

"They? Aren't you an escape artist?"

"Me? Of course not. How silly. I have trouble getting out of my own wristwatch."

"Then why does the hotel directory list you as an escapist?"

"Oh that. Those silly boobs. I'm a stagescapist, not an escapist. They left off the *s-t-a-g*."

"What the hell is a stagescapist?"

"You know what a landscapist is, don't you? Well I do the same thing, but on stage. Floral arrangements, bouquets, nosegays, that sort of thing. Many of the magicians like a background of flowers and plants. Makes it harder to see what's going on. Trees. You wouldn't happen to be in the market for a nice seven-foot ficus tree, would you? I've got an extra."

"No, Mr. Boxliner, it seems I've already spent too much time barking up the wrong one. Thanks anyway."

39

"Is this one of the Nutleys?" you ask the person with the deep voice who finally answers the phone.

"Yup."

"Which one exactly?"

"Ronnie."

"One of the twins?"

"No, the twins are busy. I'm the brother. And business manager. What's up?"

"Murder, Mr. Nutley," you announce, trying to catch him off guard. "Now, where were you last night, why aren't you listed on the hotel directory, what are the twins up to right now, and who killed Baldini? I'm waiting for your answers but be careful, this conversation is being recorded."

"Did someone kill Baldini?"

"Aha! Trying to pull the old mindless-boob ploy, eh? We've got a little bet going down here at the precinct says five-to-one *you're* the murderer. What do you say to that?"

"I'd say it would be a pretty good trick."

"Not that good, kiddo. We've got the dead man, the murderer, the motive . . . now all we need is the method.

How'd you do it? Acid in the water? Knockout drug? Tampering with the trunk lid?"

"What motive?"

"Come off it, Nutley. You think we're a bunch of morons down here? It's pretty obvious why a man like you should want to kill Henry Baldo."

"You mean because of the twins?"

"That's exactly what I mean," you say, having exactly no idea what he means. "You thought you had an airtight little plan there, didn't you? You don't register with the twins, so no one knows you're here at the hotel. They sneak you in inside a trunk then, late at night, you're free to make your move."

"According to what you're saying, the murderer had to be there to commit the crime. That lets me out."

"Oh, I'm sure you've got a swell alibi, Nut. Out all night, just got back at dawn. Plenty of witnesses. We'll unravel this charade. How about a little chat with the hotel manager about your comings and goings?"

"He won't be able to help. He's never seen me."

"Then we'll just have to find someone who has."

"Won't be easy."

"And just what makes you so sure?"

"Because I'm not at the hotel. I've never been there."

"Nice try, bucko. Suppose we send some boys down to your room and see what we can dig up?"

"I'm not at a room in the hotel. I'm downtown in my office. If the twins don't pick up after three rings, the calls are automatically forwarded."

"Oh."

"But I am intrigued by the theory that someone knocked off Baldini. If I were you guys I'd *chercher la femme*."

"No dice, pal. We're committed to this until the bitter end."

"The woman. Look for the woman. Baldini was a

woman chaser. I'll bet one of them finally turned around and chased him . . . to death."

"One of the twins maybe."

"No way. They're not his type."

"Why not?"

"Two little twelve-year-olds? Come on. Baldini may have been a bastard and a sleazebag, but he was no pervert."

40

"Fortunatus, Conjurer of the Ancients, Heir to the Secrets of the Great Selini, Magician to the Royal Family of Istanbul, Seer and Wizard, is not at home," says a recorded voice in basso profundo. "Please leave a message after the tone and the Divine Sorcerer shall return your call before the Seven Moons of Delecton have passed. Hubbaboolaba!" *Beep!*

"This is Sergeant York of the police department. . . ."

"Police?"

"Hello? Are you there?"

"Good God! Yes, I'm here. I'm monitoring calls. I can't believe this. I'm a nervous wreck. Baldini's dead and everyone thinks I did it."

The voice in person is more squeeko profundo and west enough of Istanbul to know where the Brooklyn Bridge begins.

"Why should everyone think you killed Baldini?" you continue, keeping your own persona intact.

"Because of that stupid fight we were having over the Intangible Glass routine. The papers blew that up out of all proportion. I never said I would kill him if I had the chance, for God's sake. My press agent said that.

Thought it would make good copy. Who knew Baldini was going to pull a hocus-croakus routine. God, where's my Valium?"

"What was the fight all about exactly?"

"This new trick I had invented called the Intangible Glass. I described it to one of the amateurs in the Society, a guy named Biggins. Like a jerk, I told him how it was done. Should have kept my mouth shut. What are these? These aren't Valium. Oh what the hell," he says, and gulps something down.

"What's that got to do with Baldini?"

"Well, Biggins knew Baldini too and he sold him the trick. My trick! A new gimmick is worth a lot in this business."

"Are you sure about that?"

"Sure I'm sure. I saw the props for it. It was my invention all right."

"Did it involve a sack, a crate, or a trunk?"

"No, a carpet. Why?"

"Tell me about the trick."

"It was ingenious, if I say so myself. A small wooden platform is set up in the middle of the stage and a fancy Oriental carpet is placed over it. Then a panel of glass about the size of a door is brought out. No frame, no molding, just a big thick sheet of glass. This is set up like a barrier in the middle of the platform. The magician stands on one side of the glass and a curtain is drawn around the whole setup. But the side edges and the top of the glass are left exposed so the audience can see them. When the curtain is pulled back again—presto!— the magician is on the other side of the glass. How was it done? The glass hasn't moved; the audience could see the edges all the time. There are no trick panels in the glass; the audience can examine it up close. No trapdoor in the platform; the rug would prevent entry to it. So how was it done?"

"I give up."

"Ah, here are my Valium. Cheers."

"How *was* it done?" you persist.

"That's the big secret."

"Well?" you say, settling for the answer to a lesser mystery.

"Well what?" he says, playing it coy.

"Well, you can tell me or can tell a grand jury," you say, playing a frustrated brat to absolute perfection.

"You mean I have to tell you?"

"Bingo!"

"Well, you see, there is a trapdoor in the platform, right in the middle. It sits under the glass. When it's open, it creates an eighteen-inch space under the glass for you to slip through."

"I thought the carpet prevented you from doing that."

"Normally it would, but this is a specially prepared carpet. That's my invention. It's a regular carpet with an intricate Oriental design, except for a three-foot-square section in the middle. In that middle section, the threads have been sewn onto a rubber-mat base. It stretches. You can't tell a thing looking at it from above. But once it's in place, and the door under it is open, you can stretch that part of the carpet into the space and slip through. Well, Baldini couldn't, of course. He was a fat pig. He used his assistant. You don't think I'd kill him for something as stupid as that, do you?"

"We'll see, Mr. Stuben."

"I need a drink. Where the hell is that scotch?"

"Is it so unusual for two magicians to come up with the same idea at the same time?"

"No, but this was too much of a coincidence. Besides, Baldini stole ideas and gimmicks all the time. He stole other things, too. Just ask Trixon Stage. Baldini was easy to hate. No big trick about that. He was obnoxious, overbearing, abrasive. But a lot of people had much more reason to knock him off than me. Ah, here it is! Bottoms up."

"Who, for example?"

"Dierdre Peeps. She was married to him. Horrible thought. Maybe even Noel Biggins, I don't know. Look, Sergeant, I've got to get off the phone. I'm getting a psychic message from my mentor Selini from ancient Constantinople. I'd better heed his warning."

"What warning is that?"

"That if I don't take some more Maalox real soon, I'm going to be in big trouble."

41

"Yeah?"

"Judson Wither?"

"Yeah."

"Are you aware that Henry Baldo, also known as The Great Baldini, died this morning while performing one of his tricks?"

"Aware? I bought a bottle of champagne to celebrate."

"You didn't like him very much, did you?"

"Like? Let's just say that other things were higher on my list of likes, namely bugs and warts. Baldini? He was at the top of a different list."

"Because of his relationship with your wife?"

"Ex-wife. Let's put it this way. They were perfect for each other: he was fat and she was stupid. Who is this anyway?"

"My name is Prattle, Mr. Wither. My company holds Baldini's life-insurance policy. We're trying to determine if Baldini's demise was truly an accident. You see, if it was, certain people stand to make a substantial sum of money."

"Like who?"

"Your ex-wife, for one."

"Flora? You mean that fat slob left that dumb broad money? Son-of-a-bitch. And what if it wasn't an accident?"

"Naturally, we would not be inclined to pay if there was any foul play involved."

"So what do you want from me? I didn't kill the bastard. Although I thought about it plenty of times."

"We're not suggesting that you did."

"I'm sure someone else can take the credit for it."

"For example?"

"Trixon Stage maybe. Who knows? In any case, it would have been pretty easy to pull off."

"Why?"

"Because Baldini was a pompous ass, that's why. He was so absorbed with himself, he wouldn't have noticed things. Take his props, for example. He was a fanatic about them. That alone made him vulnerable."

"How so?"

"The key to magic, Prattle, is diversion. The more someone concentrates on something over here, the easier it is to fake them out over there. You want to prove that he was murdered?"

"Sure."

"Then find out about the trick. How it was done, how it was set up, everything. Talk to one of the escape artists who knew the trick. Like Vinnie what's-his-name. Or the German guy. There's a third one too in SCAM, but I can't remember his name. When you know everything about it, look for something unusual, out of place. Some event that doesn't quite fit, that Baldini would have missed while wallowing in his own self-image. That's how you'll find your murderer."

"Well, thanks for your help."

"No problem at all. Anything I can do to screw things up for Flora is my pleasure."

44

"Oh, yes, we have no bananas. We have no bananas to*day*!"

"Excuse me," you say, having apparently interrupted a private performance with your call, "I must have the wrong number."

"Lemme tell ya something, pal. Right numbers are a dime a dozen. It's the wrong ones that count, and I should know since I *am* a count. So what's—hic—up? I mean...up."

"Is this Count Argyle?"

"Hic. Yup. Count Yabnalow Argyle, formerly of Toledo, lately of points—hic—east."

"Toledo? You're really a count from Spain?"

"Holy Toledo to you, pal. And you can always count on Spain, remember that. But I'm not talking Spain, I'm talking Toledo, Ohio. The Buckeye State. Hic. Excuse me, I seem to have developed a case of the—hic—ups."

"Are you drunk?"

"Absolutely. *Not*, that is. I am not under the affluence of inkahol as so many thinkle seem to peep. Why, do I sound drunk? Hic?"

"Were you knocking on the door of Room 34 last night at about two in the morning?"

"Two in the morning? I've been taking two in the morning for years, doesn't do a bit of good. Hic. Next question."

"Do you remember being out of your room last night? Do you remember anything? Ever?"

"Last night. Last night. Hic. I think there was a small horse loose on one of the floors. Small white horse. Yes, I was trying to milk it but it wouldn't stay put. So I returned to my room for a kitenap. That is to say—hic —a nightcap."

You begin another line of questioning but something —perhaps the low rumble of Argyle's snore—suggests that these questions too will remain unanswered.

45

"Clive, is that you?" whispers the answering voice.

"Mnnh," you say as indistinctly as you can.

"You told Gretchen to cover for us, didn't you?"

"Mnnh."

"Dumb move, babe. She's a goddamn homophobe from the year one. Should've asked me first. She's blown her top, telling everyone all about us."

"Mnnh?"

"Well, I'm just waiting for the police to call me. What should I say? I know you're on their list of suspects, babe. But if I tell them we were together all last night, you know what'll happen. I can just see the headlines: OCTOPAD STICKS IT TO THE MADAME."

"Mnnh."

"I don't care about all that. Let them find out. Maybe it would even be good publicity. I don't know. I feel nervous. Maybe Elastic Man should come down and tickle the Madame in her secret place."

"Mnnh!"

"Madame may just have to put on her Night of Pain outfit. The one with the leather garters? Come on, Oct, it's all going to come out sooner or later. Come over and whisper something nasty. I've got a brand-new boa that's never even been out of the box . . . Oct? Clive? Are you still there?"

48

"Hyman Rosen please," you say when the phone is picked up.

"This is me. Who are you?"

"My name is Weaver from Wire House Warehouse. We're on the phone today calling everyone we can about our new UltraSlim UltraStrong Grade Zero wire. Mr. Rosen, are you a man who appreciates a really fine wire?"

"Now you call. Where were you yesterday when I was breaking my neck trying to find some? Nobody wants to lend nothing. It's a good thing they had some in the basement."

"Mr. Rosen, I can promise you that if you sign up for our Total Wire program, you'll never go without it again. Now if you could just tell me exactly what you were using the wire for?"

"Levitation."

"Whose?"

"Anybody's."

"No one in particular?"

"A member of the audience."

"Oh, you use it in a trick?"

"What did you think I did with it? Floss my dentures? Of course I use it in a trick. A levitation trick."

"So you actually have to lift someone with it?"

"No, no, it's a dummy."

"How much does the dummy weigh?"

"How much does the dummy weigh! Look, you obviously have no idea what I'm talking about. So I'll explain. A person from the audience is brought up and placed on a platform. The platform rises. Someone notices thin wires holding the platform up. So I cut the wires and still the platform floats. Then I pass a hoop around the platform three times. Applause. The wires are fake; they're dummy wires. Now do you understand?"

"Can anyone else substantiate the fact that you use these wires in the trick?"

"Hah?"

"Has anyone else seen you perform this trick?"

"Sure. Everyone. It's my trademark."

"Did you know Henry Baldo?"

"Who's that?"

"The Great Baldini."

"Oh, him! I asked one of his assistants when they moved in yesterday, but they didn't have any wire either."

"In that case, Mr. Rosen, I have one last question," you say, unable to control your curiosity.

"Shoot."

"What's holding the platform up if not the wires?"

"S-bar."

"Esbar? Your assistant?"

"An S-bar. Don't know what that is, do you? It's a bar, with two bends like the letter S, that goes from a lift behind the curtain to under the platform. It lets you pass a hoop completely over the platform and, if you do it right, it frees itself on the third pass. Gives the illusion that nothing's holding the platform up. Now what about that wire?"

"What wire?"

"The UltraSuper whatever you were trying to sell me. The reason you called."

"Oh, that wire. Gee, I'm sorry, we're out of stock. In fact, we're out of business. Try Acme Wire next time. 'Bye."

50

"What ken I do f'you, honey?" says a woman with a voice like satin sheets on an unmade New Orleans bed.

"My name is Sheets," you say, overwhelmed by the sound. "You've never heard of me. . . ."

"Heard of sheets? Hell, I built a career on them."

"I'm with the Society. The official biographer."

"Well, I'm a little new to this business, babe. But if you don't mind some good raunchy sex, I'll be glad to tell you my life story."

"Actually, I'm right in the middle of Dr. Hoodoo's biography. His daughter told me that you called to warn him this morning. I thought there might be something there I should know about. You know Hoodoo well?"

"Let's just say that the doctor and me had a professional kinda relationship."

"A magic act?"

"A different kind of act. Harm—that's my little secret name for Hoodoo—worked in New Orleans for a while near my place of employment. We got to know each other real well back then."

"Where did you work?"

"Well at the cathouse, a'course."

"Is that a restaurant?"

"Honey, do I sound like a plate slinger to you? Don't you even know what a cathouse is?"

"Oh, that! But aren't you a magician?"

"I was *always* a magician. That's all I did was tricks, night 'n' day. Well, after I was busted that last time, I said to myself, I said, 'Hell, woman, this ain't no way to grow old gracefully.' So that's when I decided to take my act on the road."

"What were you warning Hoodoo about?"

"Oh, just a little somethin' I heard down in the ladies' room in the hotel lobby when I first arrived yesterday. I wasn't really warnin' him about it, just informin'. I didn't think anything of it until today when I heard about Baldini."

"What did you hear?"

"That he died, a'course."

"I mean, what did you hear in the ladies' room?"

"Well, someone came into the can and took the stall next to mine. I guess she didn't notice me, but I sure noticed her. She had on six-inch gold lamé pumps with rhinestone tips. Honey, that's my kinda shoe. Anyway, she was havin' a conversation with someone else through the wall."

"What do you mean through the wall?"

"Someone in the men's room, next door. I couldn't really make out what the man was sayin' except that he kept callin' her Befarge or Lefarge or somethin'. But I heard *her* talkin' clear enough."

"What did she say?"

"She said, and I quote this: 'Last time it *almost* killed him. Unfortunately, he came too soon. But I'll get him tonight, Beane.'"

"And you think she was referring to Baldini?" you ask, while writing the quote down.

"Like I say, I didn't think anythin' of it at the time.

But with Baldini bein' killed and all, I'm thinkin' maybe this Befarge person done it."

"But why call Hoodoo about it? Why not the police?"

"Me and the police ain't on speakin' terms, if you get my meanin'. Besides, I knew all about Hoodoo and Baldini and them bonds that was stolen."

"Hoodoo told you that?"

"Honey, the bed is better than any confessional I ever seen. Sure, he told me. He was beside himself about it, the poor ol' boy. I figured that once word got out about that, he'd be the prime suspect for havin' killed Baldini. So I thought I'd tell him about what I heard. Just so's he could protect himself if he had to. But his daughter wouldn't put old Harm on the phone."

"And you're sure about what you heard?"

"Honey, if you've ever seen Mama perform her Shootin' Ping-Pong Balls, you *know* I never tell a lie."

51

"Stuben, if you call me one more goddamn time, I'm going to come down there and show you a brand-new trick called Flattening the Nose. I'm going to tell you for the last time, I didn't sell Baldini your stupid trick. He must have found out about it from someone else. Now stop calling me, stop having your press agent call me, hang up the phone, and go back to Istanbul and charm snakes!"

"But..." you begin, trying to correct the speaker's mistaken assumption.

"But nothing, you paranoid twit. Leave me out of this insanity. Nobody's saying that Baldini was murdered. You're the only one who thinks that. The police say it was an accident."

"But—"

"Now listen to me. Go back to your shrink, tell him your delusions have started again. Get back on the medication. Do anything you goddamn want to do. Confess to the cops, for all I care. Just leave me alone!"

"But—" you try again, but this final one only butts up against the wall of silence that remains after the receiver has been slammed down.

53

"Clive Adder? This is Detective Heinz of the Fifty-seventh," you bark, hoping to shake some information loose by the assault.

"Again?"

"Again?"

"I just spoke to one of you guys. What more do you want me to tell you? Yes, I hated Baldini. Yes, I wanted to get back at him because of that Buffalo business. No, I didn't kill him. And yes, I was with Gretchen Prague all night long and she can prove it. What else is there to say?"

"Tell us one more time about the buffaloes."

"I already went through all that with Detective What's-his-name."

"Whose buffaloes were they?"

"Buffalo. The city. Baldini and I were supposed to appear there on a double bill. But he heard that I was going to do an escape trick. It wasn't really an escape, it just looked that way. I folded myself into the lid of a box and seemed to disappear from it. But Baldini didn't like competition, so he arranged to have me locked in my hotel room. I couldn't get out in time for the performance. And he started a rumor that I was a drunk who missed engagements. It's all past now, but it ruined that whole season for me."

"And that's why you—"

"I didn't kill him. Hell, I couldn't even prove he was the one who arranged the whole thing. But the way the locks were jammed, the police said only a lock expert could have done it."

"Wasn't there any other way out of the room?"

"I tried to squeeze through the air-conditioning shaft, but it was blocked."

"No windows?"

"Do you think I would have missed my performance if there was a window? Now look, I've told you everything there is to tell. If somebody killed him, it wasn't me. I wouldn't have known how. Why don't you interrogate one of the other escapists? Call up Streibnitz or the Fantôme. Or Landau. Hassle them. They'd know a lot more than I would. Okay?"

54

"Professor Bibble speaking. And who, may I ask, is calling?"

"This is Ruse from the Magicians Club."

"Magicians Club? Now let me see. You know I've appeared at almost every registered magical club and society in the country; in fact I'm considering submitting my lecture schedule to the *Guinness Book of Records.* But in all honesty I must say I'm not familiar with your group. You say it's called . . ."

"Magicians Club. Strictly amateur, Professor. We're basically just a bunch of guys and gals that really dig magic. We're doing a benefit next month, wondered if you'd like to come and talk to our little group. Very informal, tea and Danish, that sort of thing. What do you say?"

"Well, I do give talks and seminars on the history of magic. That is, after all, my expertise. I cover magical history all the way from tribal shamanism up to the great magicians of the Golden Age at the turn of the century. Thurston, Houdini, Nate Leipsig, Max Malini. I also perform examples of their work. Now, of course as you no doubt have heard, certain of the forebears of modern magic—"

"Great, it's a deal. Now, Prof—is it okay if I call you Prof?—a lot of our members are especially interested in escapes. You know, Houdini, Baldini. Can you possibly tailor your talk to that specialty."

"Oh, well, certainly. Escape magic is, naturally, among the most spectacular of all effects, combining as it does the talents of both daredevil and dramatist. And in no one were these two abilities better balanced than in the greatest escape artist of all, Harry Houdini. Now Houdini as you probably know, whose real name was Erich Weiss, was born—"

"Yup, they sure don't make them like Houdini anymore!"

"Well, that's quite true; but equally true is the fact that newer forms of entertainment such as motion pictures and television have removed some of the mystery and aura of stage magic. Rare is the performer these days who can compete with the large-scale magical effects that one sees—"

"Except say for The Great Baldini."

"Yes, well, perhaps, but of course history will be the final judge there. And I must say that although there are now some fine escape artists such as Le Grand Fantôme and The Elusive Streibnitz, or Landau the Impossible, none of them can truly compare in my judgment to the simpler delights of, say, a Max Malini. Now, have I mentioned that many years ago, as a small and somewhat naïve young fellow interested in magic, this was in Brooklyn in the early Twenties, I had the great honor to meet Malini himself. Yes, it was a cold November day, I recall very well, and I was returning home from school. . . ."

55

"Connie Deirdre?" you inquire, but the sounds of the answer are drowned out by a loud crash, the thud of the phone being dropped, then a second crash, and, finally, a woman frantically shouting louder than her own fist pounding on the wall of the hotel room.

"Laurie! Get the hell in here! The damn goat is choking on my shoes. *Laurie!*"

56

"Hello hello!" squawks a high-pitched voice into the receiver. "Tickle your ass with a feather?"

"Hello?"

"Hello hello! I said particularly nasty weather."

"Is this Laurie Delbingo?"

"Hello hello! *Awk!* His wife looks like an otter."

"I must have the wrong number."

"Awk! I said his life is like no other."

"Thanks anyway," you say, wondering how you managed to dial the local asylum by accident.

"Bad boy," shouts a new voice on the line. "Go back to your perch. I never should have taught you to answer the phone. Bad boy. Hello? Are you still there?"

"I'm not sure."

"Sorry about that. Caspar gets a little carried away with himself sometimes. This is Laurie Delbingo. Can I help you with something?"

"Was that a parrot?"

"Cockatoo."

"Smart bird."

"Not smart enough. Look, I hate to be rude, but Beatrice just took a dump all over the mirror. Bad girl, Beatrice. You looking for an animal trainer or something?"

"No, a witness."

"You getting married?"

"I'm looking into The Great Baldini's accidental death this morning."

"Ah, insurance investigator. So what do you want from me? Bennie, put down that hair-dryer right now! Back in the cage. Don't give me that look. I dried your hair yesterday."

"You've trained one of your birds to use a hair-dryer?"

"Bennie's a chimp. Caspar and Beatrice are the birds. So you need info on Baldini, is that it?"

"Exactly."

"Like what? I didn't really know him."

"Did you happen to see him moving in yesterday or at any time since?"

"Yeah, I saw him a few times when I moved in. Down at the front desk, in the hallway. I didn't pay much attention to him. I was too busy with the cages."

"For your animals?"

"Two dogs, one chimp, two birds, one goat, and Murray."

"Your husband?"

"Companion."

"Human?"

"Is this conversation private?"

"Sure."

"Murray's a Shetland pony. White with brown ears. Very cute. The kids go crazy over him. I'm supposed to leave him down in the stockroom. There's some jackass ruling about having horses in the rooms. But Murray gets lonely down there. So last night I sneaked him upstairs and kept him in the room with me."

"I see."

"Somehow, in the middle of the night, Murray opened the door to the room and got out. I had to chase him all over the place. I finally found that drunk Count Argyle trying to molest him on the third floor. Bennie! Turn that TV off and go take a nap!"

"So you didn't notice anything suspicious or unusual?"

"I don't know what you call suspicious, but that man was trying to rape my horse. That ain't normal."

"I mean anything unusual regarding Baldini."

"Help! Help! She's killing me!"

"Hello?"

"She's boring me to death! It's torture!"

"Are you all right?"

"Caspar, you idiot, get off the extension. Bad boy."

"Ms. Delbingo?"

"Stop her before it's too late! Awk!"

"Go back to your cage. No, I didn't notice anything else. Ask that guy Magic What's-his-name. Magic Milkman or Mullman. He knew Baldini better than I did. Bennie! Damn it! Get your head out of the toilet!"

57

"Yo, what's up?"

"I'd like to speak to Drew Scriver," you say.

"So speak."

"Drew Scriver, the technician for SCAM."

"Right."

"Is that you?"

"So far."

"But you're a woman."

"That's what my folks kept telling me. Now look, pal, being a woman named Drew is my little problem, but what exactly is *your* problem? I'm a little busy here. I've got a scaffold to finish, a six-foot Jack of Clubs to mount, and two levitation platforms to paint before the Ball."

"A scaffold?"

"The Amazing Mingus hangs himself in full view of the audience, then comes back to life seven inches taller than before. Now what's on your mind?"

"Did you work on any of the props for Henry Baldo?"

"Baldini? No way. He used freelancers. Once they were constructed, Baldini never let anybody touch his props. I mean I occasionally fixed something if it was broke, but that's it. He was paranoid about his stuff."

"Why?"

"Afraid someone would sabotage it, I guess. Looks like that someone succeeded."

"Oh really?"

"No, O'Reilly. Cab O'Reilly, the card guy."

"How do you know that?"

"He was down in the shop the day before yesterday asking all sorts of questions. What you might call suspicious questions."

"Like?"

"Like how could you fix it so someone couldn't get out of the canvas-bag trick. That kind of thing."

"The canvas-bag trick? That was part of Baldini's routine."

"Natch. It's a basic escape. Houdini did it, too. You slit the real inside hem and sew it up again. Big deal."

"What did you tell him?"

"Houdini? Never met the man."

"O'Reilly."

"Really. Why, did you ever meet him?"

"I mean . . . did you tell O'Reilly about a way to sabotage the trick?"

"Plenty of ways to do it. He cuts the fake hem with a razor stashed in his mouth, right? Switch it for a stage razor. You know, one without a sharp edge. Luther Rebob sells that kind of junk. Then he can't cut his way out. Trapped in the bag. Underwater? Dead. That's how I'd do it."

"Would you?"

"Do it? Nah. I had nothing against Baldini personally, except that he was a loud, fat slob. But Cab there . . . now that's a different story."

"What *is* the story?"

"Not my place to say, pal. Let's just say Baldini stole something of Cab's."

"A trick?"

"A wife."

"Oh really?"

"No, O'Reilly. Connie O'Reilly."

58

"Elena, is that you?" Ollie Bemble says cautiously upon answering the phone.

"Yup," you mumble, ever ready to take advantage of mistaken identity.

"Thanks for calling back. I had to talk to someone. I don't know what the hell is going on. Last night, Harman asked me to do a simple favor for him. I was to wait in the hallway outside Room 34 while Woody Beams brought Baldini's props in. No big deal, right?"

"Yup."

"All Harman wanted me to do was to accidentally spill a glass of gin on the canvas sack. Not the boxes, not the suitcases, not the other bags. Just the canvas sack. A whole glass of gin. Harman said it was a practical joke. I didn't really get the joke but I did it because he asked me to. No harm done, right?"

"Yup."

"I mean, who likes gin anyway besides that crazy rabbit that Duke uses in his act? You know the rabbit I'm talking about, right? Dr. Plato called me before to ask me if I'd seen it. It's missing. How should I know where the Duke's rabbit is? That's not my problem, right?"

"Yup."

"Anyway, yesterday I did just what Harman asked me to do. I went down to Room 34 and waited until they brought the props in. Then Argyle came along and he was drinking too, so it made it look even more innocent. I stood around and waited until Woody carried the sack in, then I made believe that Argyle bumped into me and I spilled the glass of gin all over the sack. Hell, I don't even drink gin. You know that."

"Yup."

"Then this morning I find out that Baldini's been killed while performing the Triple Escape. Killed! I mean the sack was part of the trick. You don't think it had anything to do with . . . I mean, I called Harman, but he's not taking any calls. But it's impossible, right? Some gin spilled on something can't kill someone. It's not possible. Right?"

"Nope."

60

"Edna Parofin speaking. May I help you?"

"You're Madame X, aren't you?"

"That's one of my names, yes. My fans call me Madame X. My friends call me Edna. The Internal Revenue insists on calling me Mrs. Parofin, even though I've never been married. And my mother, of course, calls me Lucy, but that's simply because she's senile. Now which group do you fit in?"

"None, Madame. My name is Kline from the Institute for Advanced Study of Weird Phenomena. . . . "

"Oh yes, I've heard of your organization."

"You have?"

"Aren't you the people who investigated the Shroud of New Brunswick last year?"

"Yes, that's us, all right! Well then, I'm sure you know why we're calling."

"For a donation?"

"No, but we do need your help. As you no doubt know by now, Henry Baldo died this morning."

"Oh, yes. I knew it was coming."

"You did, did you?"

"I saw it in the papers yesterday."

"In the papers? But it only happened today. No one outside this hotel could know about it yet. Which papers did you see it in?"

"The Post-It notes."

"I'm sorry, Madame, we must just be talking about two completely different things here. Please tell me we're talking about two different things."

"Henry Baldo's premature demise. Yes?"

"Yes. But Post-It notes? I really don't see how they fit in."

"It's a future-telling technique I use. It's impossible to get authentic tea leaves these days, so I've discovered that Post-It notes serve just as well. I burn a pad—the white ones work best—and can read the future from the ashes. I knew Henry Baldo was going to get himself into some trouble and indeed he has."

"Oh boy."

"And I'm sure that Hector Vell is feeling terrible about his curse."

"Excuse me?"

"Hector asked me to put a curse on Henry Baldo. I usually don't do that kind of thing, but when I heard the reason, I agreed. I'm an old-fashioned woman, you see. So I pierced a photograph of Henry Baldo with the Seven Needles of Mystic Retribution. Then just yesterday I burned the papers to see what the result might be and guess what they showed? Poor Baldini with a terrible allergy attack."

"An allergy attack? You mean like a runny nose?"

"More like asthma."

"Bad enough to kill him?"

"Oh no! My curse had nothing to do with that. The Seven Needles could never be fatal. They can only induce a slight irritation, like a large pimple, for instance, right on the tip of the nose. They're very mild. Would you like a demonstration sometime?"

"That definitely won't be necessary. Thanks for your help with our investigation."

"Anytime. If you'd like, I could pass three candles over the toilet at noon."

"Fine, fine. Anything you say."

"That will ensure success in your efforts. The toilet at full flush being the only equivalent of a waterfall in this vicinity."

"Naturally."

"Well, I'm off then. I have an incantation to do first, if I can find a cat without offspring and a pair of galoshes never worn."

"Yes, well. Goodbye then. And good luck."

"Luck, my dear, is the fool's name for fate."

61

"Duke Melenetti?"

"Yeah, speaking. Are you calling about Waldo?"

"Waldo?"

"My rabbit. Harman borrowed him last night and now he can't find him. He's not even answering the phone anymore."

"Waldo?"

"No, Harman. His daughter says she thinks he got loose in the hotel."

"Harman got loose?"

"Waldo, you moron. Try and follow. Waldo is my rabbit. Okay so far? Harman Hoodle borrowed him last night. When I called to get him back, Harman said he got loose in the hotel somewhere. I've been calling all around trying to find out if anyone's seen him. Understand? Now I take it that's not why you're calling."

"A white rabbit?"

"Brown with beige spots."

"Sorry."

"Look, if you do see him, you've got to nab him for me and bring him back. I'm sunk without him. But don't lunge for him or make loud noises. That'll just scare him and he'll run away. He's got sensitive ears. There's a special way to get him to come to you."

"Make sounds like a carrot?"

"Funny. I'll throw that into my act. No, just get some gin, put it in a glass or a dish, and place it inside a bag or a box."

"Gin? Did you say gin?"

"He's been trained to follow the scent of gin. He finds the source of the smell and then sits there until he's called back. Especially if it's inside an enclosure. He likes dark places."

"Does the ASPCA know about your act?"

"Sure. I treat him good."

"How about Alcoholics Anonymous?"

"Look, he doesn't drink it. He just sits near it and sniffs. It works great. See, I put him in a top hat on one side of the stage, and while I'm talking he slips out the bottom and follows the scent of gin behind the curtain to another hat on the other side of the stage. He climbs in and waits. It's automatic. He does it all by himself. Great little hare."

"And you say Harman Hoodle borrowed him for the night?"

"Yeah. Now what the hell Harman wanted him for I'll never know. He doesn't do animal tricks. But look, he's been real nice to my sister Elena, so I let him borrow Waldo. Now he's gone and lost him. Just great. Now remember, if you see him, some gin inside a sack or box. Okay?"

62

"Hello. Simon Penn speaking."

"Mr. Penn," you begin, struggling for a convincing identity, "this is Woodward of the *Washington Post*."

"*The* Woodward?"

"No, the other Woodward. We're doing a story on Baldini's Triple Escape and we'd like to get a complete description of the trick for our piece."

"Obit?"

"You bet. Did you ever see it performed?"

"Baldini never really performed the whole trick before an audience. But he described it to me and showed me parts of it for our newsletter. It's three different escapes, one inside the other. But let me tell you something: the real scoop is that he stole most of it from other escapists."

"Would you mind telling us exactly how the trick was supposed to go?"

"Sure thing. Do I get a credit?"

"A college credit?"

"Hah."

"Huh?"

"Come on, I'm not going to give out all this information without a mention in the piece."

"Oh, that kind of credit. Absolutely. Right at the front."

"Great. That's Simon Penn, with two *n*'s."

"Well shoot . . . with two *o*'s."

"Okay. Baldini is handcuffed, then placed in a large canvas sack, like a mailbag. Members of the audience have already inspected it to make sure it's legitimate. Once he's inside, the opening is tied and secured with leather straps and ropes. Elapsed time, three minutes."

"Got it."

"There's a small hoist on the stage, like the kind they use to raise car motors. With it, his assistant hoists up the sack and puts it into a wooden crate that's also been inspected by the audience. A wooden lid is nailed on, then a thick rope is tied all around the crate—giftbox style—so all the sides are roped in. All this takes about five more minutes."

"Check."

"While that's being done, a larger metal trunk is being inspected and filled with water. It's a heavy-duty trunk, made of steel or something, with rivets and things. Very impressive, I've seen it. When it's completely filled with water, the wooden crate is lowered into it. Air bubbles form on the surface as the water in the trunk rushes in to fill the crate. The steel lid of the trunk is put in place and secured to metal clasps on the collar of the trunk with four heavy padlocks. This part with the trunk takes another six minutes. You getting all this down?"

"Roger."

"Simon. Now check out this last part. A tall screen, like a shower curtain on wheels, is placed around the trunk and the curtain is closed. Baldini's assistant leads the audience in counting down from twenty. At the end of that countdown, the curtain is pulled back and—lo and behold—the trunk is still sitting there just like before. No change. You figure Baldini's been trapped for about sixteen minutes, and completely underwater for about six of those minutes."

"Wow."

"Okay, big panic. No one can live that long underwater. The assistant quickly unlocks the locks, removes the steel lid from the trunk, attaches the hoist to the crate inside, and pulls it out, water pouring all over the place. The crate is set down. Everything is still intact. Observers on stage knock frantically on the box to make sure he's still alive, but there's no sound from inside. The ropes are cut, the wooden lid is removed with a crowbar, the audience is in a panic. Should I slow down?"

"No."

"Inside the crate is the sack, still roped and buckled. They open it up and inside find only the empty handcuffs and a note saying that the show looks good from row seventeen. Finally, to the shock and delight of all present, Baldini—the exact same Baldini they handcuffed almost twenty-five minutes before—reveals himself to be sitting in row seventeen in the middle of the auditorium. Da-*da*!"

"Holy mackerel!"

"Not bad, huh?"

"How did he do it?"

"That, my friend, is the story of the year. Even if I knew, I couldn't put it in the newsletter. That's taboo."

"How could I find out how it was done?"

"Another escapist maybe. There are rumors that Baldini stole each of the parts of the trick from other performers. But I'd be surprised if they give away any secrets. Magicians don't like reporters much. After all, news is about revealing things; magic is about what's hidden. See what I mean?"

You do exactly, and return to your list of names with a firm commitment to deceit.

64

"Hello? What can I do for you?"

"Amazing Mingus?"

"That's me. You can just call me Amazing. All my friends do. Except that Mr. Argyle, a real schlemiel who insists on calling me Seagull for reasons unknown. And to whom do I have the pleasure of speaking?"

"I'm a private investigator, Mr. Amazing—"

"No, you miss my point. Let me try to make it clear. It's Mr. Seigel or Amazing. No Mr. Amazing, no Mr. Mingus, no Mr. Magician. Either Mr. Seigel or Amazing. Those are the choices. Kapeesh?"

"Yes. Fine. As I said, I'm looking into—"

"I know, I know. You've been hired by the hotel—which is hoping to avoid unpleasant publicity—to look into the death this morning of Henry Baldo to ascertain whether or not any foul play was involved."

"Amazing!"

"Yes?"

"You hit the nail on the head."

"A carpenter I'm not. A man of average intelligence who can see two feet in front of his nose, I am. Now, let me further predict that you're calling me in relation to that ridiculous bet I waged with a certain Mr. Cab O'Reilly as to the possible methods of eliminating the unfortunate Mr. Baldo. Yes?"

"Exactly."

"And you wish to know whether or not Mr. O'Reilly was capable of actually carrying out his nefarious plan. Or whether indeed I, having heard of his method, may not have had my own designs for switching a false razor blade into Mr. Baldo's bag of tricks. Thus causing him to drown before he could effect his escape. Equally correct?"

"Yes."

"Then to be blunt, may I say that you have not exactly done your homework on this project and that further inquiry—a call for example to Woodrow the prop assistant—will establish that this method was not used because the killer would not have been so stupid as to leave such an obvious clue."

"Oh."

"And if I may further speculate, it will soon become plain that the more desirable method would be the one which leaves no evidence whatsoever. You should be looking, may I be so bold to suggest, for some minor event, something slightly out of the ordinary that Baldo and his assistants would not notice in their endeavor to protect the precious props. Do I make myself clear?"

"Yes, but—"

"So don't sit there examining your pupik all morning. Get on the phone and find out all you can about the activities surrounding the props in the hours preceding Mr. Baldo's practice session. And don't be offended by my French. A pupik is a navel. Hello?"

"What makes *you* think he was murdered?"

"Why not? It's a reasonable assumption based on his dubious character. The man was a gonif. You know what a gonif is? It's someone who not only breaks the commandment to steal, but while he's at it he also steals the

Bible itself. That's your Mr. Baldo. And there's another
good reason for you to look further into the possibility
that he was murdered."

"Yes?"

"You got something better to do?"

65

"Sherlock Holmes?" you inquire, not quite sure what to expect.

"Just a moment," says the voice as strings on an instrument are plucked and tuned. "Now."

"I'm . . . um . . . doing . . . um . . . some—what should I call it—investigating into the —"

"Come, come now. Who you are and what you are doing are self-evident, as obvious as the moon. Let's do get on with it. You are Edgar Poole's cousin, a mystery writer, and you're trying to determine who killed Henry Baldo. But you're stumped on how the murderer was able to do it and so you've looked in the hotel directory, found my name, and called hoping that I, like my namesake, would be able to afford some insight. Am I correct in these assumptions?"

"Amazing, Holmes. How did you know all that? Was it elementary?"

"Not at all, it took damn hard figuring. Your very first statement—'Sherlock Holmes?' with a blush of disbelief —told me that we had never met before and you weren't certain who or what I was. Since everyone in SCAM knows me, I concluded that you must be from outside the Society, either a hotel worker or a new amateur. I recalled Edgar telling me he couldn't make it this year and was sending his cousin, a mystery writer, to take his place and so I correctly surmised that you were that person. Furthermore, as a mystery writer, you could not help but be taken in by this morning's challenge and the rest follows logically."

"But how did you know I was stumped on how the murderer—"

"The challenge of any crime is twofold: method and motive. Since the murderer in this case was obviously a magician, I infer that the method used must have been rather tricky, deceptive. That is, after all, a magician's forte. This, therefore, is the logical stumbling block."

"So you think he was murdered, too?"

"An assumption of murder always has a fruitful life span, even if it itself dies a natural death."

"But how was it done?"

"To the trained mind, the incidentals leave a trail as clear as mud in the snow. Look to the details. I will add one thing, though. I have always considered that one of medicine's peripheral intrigues could be effectively incorporated into a murder scheme."

"Yes?"

"The whole area of allergies. Here one encounters perfectly natural trauma of a fatal kind. Particularly bronchial reactions, which are almost indistinguishable from other anaphylactic responses. True, an autopsy would divulge the existence of histamines and perhaps even the allergen itself, but if there were another possible cause of death, these might be overlooked as trivial."

"Allergies. You think maybe Baldini was killed by ragweed?"

"Or worse."

"Goldenrod?"

"Broaden your thinking. Fluids? Drugs? Animals? Man is a sensitive creature. Anyway, it's just a suggestion. And now, if you'll permit me, I must get back to practicing for tonight's performance."

"Violin?"

"A distant cousin—the banjo."

"Sherlock Holmes playing the banjo?"

"I know. I've tried to learn the violin for the sake of authenticity, but I just can't seem to get the hang of it," he says, and ends the interview with a jazzy flourish.

"This is Hazel Wolman. May I help you?"

"My name is Travelers. From the insurance company? Division seven, unit three, magic claims. We're looking into a claim regarding Henry Baldo, alias The Great Baldini."

"What kind of claim?"

"Apparently there was some sort of commotion at Mandrake's Bar in Chicago a while back involving Mr. Baldo. Our client, an innocent bystander, fractured her foot. Were you present during this episode?"

"Which one?"

"Was there more than one?"

"When Baldini's involved there's always a commotion. Jilted lovers, cuckolded husbands, scam victims. Baldini was quite a showman. Two weeks ago, for example, Calvin Quinz came charging into the bar and walloped him. He said Baldini stole five thousand dollars from him. Personally, I'm rather surprised that anyone ever trusts the man in the first place. In any case, he fractured Baldini's nose. I'm also a nurse, so I took care of him when it happened. Is that the episode you're talking about?"

"Sounds like it. Did the term *cony* come up at all?"

"Oh that episode. No, the cony episode was two months ago. Also at Mandrake's. But that one, I'm afraid, was my fault."

"Did you have something against Baldini as well?"

"No, it was a total accident. I had no idea he was allergic."

"Come again?"

"Well, you see, I went to Mandrake's that night wearing my fur coat. I hardly ever wear it, but I did that night. It's a gorgeous coat. I sat down at a table right next to Baldini. He was with Trixon Stage's wife. She loved the coat too and asked me what kind it was. I told her it was a cony coat."

"What kind?"

"Rabbit. A cony is a rabbit. So I held it up to Baldini's face so he could see it closely. Well, I thought he was going to die. He turned quite blue and started gasping for breath. It was quite horrible. We had to call the emergency medical service to administer oxygen and, eventually, epinephrine."

"What's that?"

"Adrenaline, to help him breathe."

"You're saying he almost died simply because he was allergic to your rabbit-fur coat?"

"Oh, yes. Some allergies can be quite serious. Ask any doctor. Is any of this information helpful for your investigation?"

"Duke, if that's you, just listen. I can't hold the phone right now. My hands are full of chemicals. I'm cooking up a new batch of Magic Volcanic Mix and if I miss the boiling point, it'll blow up on me. Now I made a few calls about Waldo, but I haven't located him yet. No one's seen him. But as soon as I finish this, I promise I'll get on top of it. Don't worry. Just give me another ten minutes and we'll find out what's happened to Waldo. Okay, sport?"

71

"That is it, Clive! No more calls! You are going to get me into trouble over this stupid affair. Five people, including a policeman, have already called me to find out if we were together last night. The entire hotel is on the phone discussing our torrid love tryst. Well, I am not going to cover for you anymore. I refuse to be your little excuse for one more minute. Find another alibi for your whereabouts last night and leave me out of it!"

"But—"

"Do not interrupt! If anyone else calls, I tell them the truth. I tell them you were with Peter last night, not me. And let your precious reputation suffer the consequences. Let the whole world know that the famous Octopad is a homosexual. It isn't my concern. Don't you realize that people think Baldini was murdered? Everybody's questioning everyone else. This has all gotten quite out of hand. We're not lovers, we've never been lovers, and I'm not going to pretend that we were simply so you can save face. I don't know why I agreed to it in the first place!"

73

"Yeah, hey, who is this? What's going on?"

"Magic Millikan?"

"Yeah, right, Magic Millikan. Mike, call me Mike. Hey, what's the deal here? Nobody's called me for three months, now just because I knew Baldini I'm a big celebrity. Hey, what the hell, right? Maybe it'll lead to a few gigs."

"How well *did* you know Baldini?"

"Hey, the guy and me were like Siamese twins connected at the back. We never saw each other. Hey, that's a joke. Get it?... Anyway, yeah, I knew Baldini. We shared a few snorts down at Mandrake's now and again. Never talked magic, though."

"Why not?"

"Hey, I wouldn't trust that guy as far as I could piss beer. You know what I mean? He'd sooner steal your act than buy the second round. Big ladies' man, too."

"So what *did* you talk about?"

"How the hell should I know? You think I was listening? Hey, you're not too big on gags, are you? Ever see me do the Farting Ace of Diamonds routine? It's a crack-up."

"Let's get to the point, Mike. What do *you* think happened this morning?"

"The sun rose and my wife had cramps. Do I win?"

"Baldini."

"Oh, that! Hey, I knew someone was going to pop off the old guy sooner or later. Everyone hated him. Did you talk to Trixon Stage? Or any of the escape guys? Listen, for the right price I would have rigged the cuffs. And I come cheap!"

"Rigged what cuffs?"

"The handcuffs. Didn't Baldini use them in his act? According to Arlo Sandow, it's easy to do. Arlo used to do this bar trick down at Mandrake's. No one could get out of the cuffs, even with the key. Hey, you ever been to Mandrake's?"

"Did this Arlo Sandow have anything against Baldini?"

"Hey, I told you, everyone had something against him. He was a bigmouth. You know, a brag. Derry Dilman just told me someone had threatened to kill him."

"Derry who?"

"Dilman. I was just on the phone with her. She overheard someone planning to kill Baldini."

"Did you report this to the police?"

"I am. Aren't you the police? Hey, that reminds me. Did you ever hear the joke about the cop with the three-foot dingdong?"

"Yes."

76

"This is great. This is the most exciting thing since Gaspar Fanatol choked to death on the Catch a Bullet in the Teeth routine three years ago. Were you with us then?"

"Olivia Fray?"

"Of course Gaspar was a sweetheart. He was mourned deeply. It was quite a horrendous scene, too. Oscar Fore trying to Heimlich the .44-caliber bullet out of his throat while poor Gaspar turned seven shades of blue. My God, I remember it like it was yesterday."

"Miss Fray..."

"But Baldini, now that's a different matter entirely. It's not exactly a tragedy, if you don't mind my saying so. Four different magicians accused him of blatantly stealing tricks from them. And three others named him in adultery suits. Not that I can see what those women saw in him. To me he resembled nothing so much as a ham hock with a mustache. But there you are."

"Olivia..."

"I'm not saying that any of them actually killed him, mind you. But they certainly had good reason to try. Take Judson Wither, for example. His wife Flora had been carrying on with Baldini for months. It was in all the newspapers. Just imagine how humiliated Judson felt. Why, I would have killed Baldini myself if I had been in Judson's shoes. Wouldn't you?"

"Well . . ."

"Nevertheless, I'm sure Judson meant only to scare Baldini and not actually murder him. That is, if he had anything to do with the accident at all. And I'm not saying he did, mind you. I'm just speculating. But after all, Judson does know Dierdre and she wasn't what you would call an unconcerned party either."

"Excuse me . . ."

"Oh, that's perfectly all right. I should get off the phone as well. I can't simply gossip all day. I've got three more decks to mark. But I simply must call Circe and tell her my theory about Judson. Gwendolyn loves this kind of thing. It's been lovely talking to you, and if I hear anything further on these matters, I'll be sure and give you a call."

77

"Is this Derry Dilman?" you ask when the phone has been answered.

"Yes, it is. Is this the police?"

"Sure," you say, taking advantage of the error.

"Well, I'm glad you finally called back. I didn't want to say anything in public, so I thought I'd tell you what I know over the phone."

"That's fine, Ms. Dilman. Now what exactly do you know?"

"Well, I'm staying in Room 77. Last night I was awakened about midnight by a terrible fight that was taking place in the room above mine, Room 87."

"Go on."

"Now don't get the impression that I'm an eavesdropper, but I did listen carefully to what was said. There were two voices—a high-pitched squeaky one and a deeper gruff one. They were arguing furiously for about an hour. Very insulting to each other, very nasty."

"Does this have anything to do with anything, Ms. Dilman?"

"I'm just getting to that. They were arguing over plans for something. Whether to do something by a certain date or whether to forget it. Then I heard the higher voice say something like, 'I can't take it anymore. I'm going to kill you, Baldini!' "

"I see. And then?"

"The argument continued for a while, back and forth, then it became more subdued, then I went to sleep."

"And what exactly do you make of all this, Ms. Dilman?"

"I didn't make anything of it at the time. But now that Baldini's dead, it's all obvious. Baldini went up to visit the person in Room 87, they had a disagreement, and whoever is staying in that room killed him."

"But Baldini was found dead in a locked trunk this morning."

"That's easy to explain. That person drugged him. A slow-acting drug that only hit him once he was inside the trunk. Maybe it was even something activated by what Baldini had for breakfast. I saw that once on television. Then he'd get into the trunk, pass out, take in water, drown. The perfect murder."

"And do you have any idea why someone might want to do such a thing, Ms. Dilman?"

"I've heard the same rumors as everyone else."

"Such as?"

"Baldini's second greatest ability—after escapes— was escapades. Sexual escapades. There were a lot of husbands who would have liked the Triple Escape to be his last trick. Just ask Harlan Kellogg. He knows what I mean."

78

"Don't say anything! Don't say a word, let me guess," says the voice answering the call. "You're from . . . from *Magician's Magazine* . . . and you want me to renew my subscription!"

"No."

"I knew that, I knew that. Only kidding. So tell me . . . Dr. Febrund . . . when do you want to change the appointment for?"

"This isn't Dr. Febrund."

"Dr. Withers?"

"Wrong again."

"Are you with the phone company?"

"Are *you* Harlan Kellogg?" you counter.

"Gee, my ESP seems to be slightly off kilter today. Usually I get it right on the first try. Maybe there's too much moisture in the air. If it's very wet out, I can't see too clearly through the third eye."

"I'd like to ask you some questions regarding Henry Baldo."

"Who?"

"The Great Baldini."

"Oh, him. Didn't know him too well. Only met him

once. In the Catskills. We were both performing. But he wasn't too fond of mind readers. Mind you, I wasn't getting paid for it. I'm just an amateur. It was a charity thing."

"What do you know about him?"

"Just that he screwed around. Everybody knows that. But I can predict it before it happens. I even warned Aladdin last year that his wife was going to have an affair with Baldini."

"Who's Aladdin?"

"He's here this year. Don't know his real name. He's the one that does the trick with the three watermelons and the bicycle pump. He said he'd kill Baldini if it happened. Well, it happened. Guess it was just a figure of speech. I also predicted it with Trixon Stage's wife. Just between you and me, I can't understand what these women see in Baldini."

"Saw."

"Does he saw them? I guess that turns some women on. There's no accounting for taste."

"What these women *saw* in Baldini. He's dead. Didn't you know that?"

"What? You're kidding! When did that happen?"

"This morning. As he was practicing his Triple Water Escape."

"No kidding. Landau always told me these escapes were dangerous. Landau was an escapist once himself. But I thought it was all just hype. That's terrible news."

"Is it?"

"It sure is. I should have known."

"Why is that?"

"ESP. I've been sitting here all morning trying to bring something to mind, you know, to tune in some ambient brain waves. All I keep getting is tuna fish."

"Tuna fish?"

"Yes, a strong tuna message. Very mysterious."

"Maybe you're just hungry."

"Of course! That's it! Sandy packed a tuna sandwich for the train ride and I never got to eat it. It's still in my suitcase. That explains it! Case closed."

"Great. Well, thanks for your help. I'll just be saying—"

"Wait, wait. Don't tell me, let me guess. I *know* what you're about to say. Just a minute. I'm getting it. I'm getting it. Is it . . . goodbye?"

"Right."

"I knew it!"

80

"Mr. Valentine, this is—"

"I know, I know. You're the detective in charge of the Baldini case and you're calling to find out what I know about it."

"Well actually—"

"I'll tell you exactly what I told the cops when they were here this morning. All I know is what Ollie Bemble told me. He used to work for Baldini and Harman Hoodle when they had a business together a while back. Hoodle thought that Baldini robbed him of some kind of savings bonds or something."

"Mr. Valentine—"

"That's all I know. Honest. Does that mean that Hoodle killed Baldini? Who knows? But I'll tell you this: if he did, Ollie had nothing to do with it. Ollie's a nice guy. Talk to him yourself. I'm sure he's got nothing to hide."

"Is there anything—"

"That's all I can tell you. I've got to go and get ready for the Ball tonight. I'm going to make a member of the audience disappear right from the seat. By the way, I do police benefits all the time if you've got one coming up. That's Terry Valentine, not to be confused with that jerk of a brother of mine who calls himself Ronzoni. Okay? Give me a call."

81

"Terry Valentine?"

"Yup."

"O'Hare from the Friends of Rabbits. We understand that you are the owner of one of our furry little friends."

"Not me, pal. I don't use rabbits. My act is strictly vegetarian."

"Are you sure?"

"Absolutely. I juggle six bananas during the Garden of Eden routine. I cut open a watermelon for the Reappearing Watch trick. And sometimes, if things are really slow, I resort to Six Apples in a Washtub. But that's it. In other words, no meat."

"But we were told that you sometimes used a rabbit in your act."

"You're thinking of my brother Jerry. He had a rabbit for a while. Used to stuff him up his sleeve, then toss him into a burning pan."

"Why would he do something as bizarre as that?"

"It's a trick. You know, he shows both sides of the silk, then pulls the rabbit out of his sleeve. Then he tosses the bugger in the fondue pan, puts the lid on, and —presto!—the rabbit's gone."

"Where does it go?"

"It's still in the lid. The lid and the pan liner pull out together. Standard gimmick."

"Your brother doesn't do this trick anymore?"

"No. The last time he tried it, the lid got stuck and the rabbit fried."

"My God, that's terrible! What did he do?"

"What could he do? He made a stew."

"Well, this is certainly something I must report to my supervisor."

"Sure, but tell your supervisor to tenderize it first. Otherwise it gets pretty stringy."

83

"Nostradamus the Second at your service. I know all, I see all, I understand all, and I can guess the rest. Who is this? Whadaya want?"

"Shouldn't *you* be able to tell me?"

"Gimme a break, pal. I don't go on stage until nine-thirty tonight."

"I'm calling about Henry Baldo."

"Then you got the wrong number."

"Why is that?"

"'Cause this ain't Henry Baldo, that's why. This is Nostradamus the Second, whose vision extends to the four corners of time and space."

"What do you know *about* Henry Baldo?"

"About as much as I know about you. Nothin'. If you're so curious about Baldo, why don't you call him up and stop bothering me."

"The Great Baldini is dead."

"No shit? You're kidding."

"You didn't know?"

"Never heard a word."

"There are even rumors that he was murdered."

"Holy canoli. Who did it?"

"Why don't you peer into the four corners of time and space and tell me."

"Very funny."

"You're supposed to be a clairvoyant. What does the future tell you?"

"Cut the bullshit. The only thing the future tells me is that taxes will rise and my arches will fall. But what's Baldini's murder got to do with me?"

"Your name has come up."

"Mine? Impossible. I never met the dude."

"There are no other Waldos in the Society."

"Except the rabbit."

"Which rabbit?"

"Waldo the rabbit. Duke Melenetti owns it. Uses it in one of his tricks. It's trained to follow the scent of gin. Weird as hell. Who mentioned my name in connection with Baldini anyway? Hello? Hello?"

85

"Clara Forme speaking."

"Are you the veterinarian for SCAM?"

"I am."

"Great. I'm Katz from the ASPCA. We're doing some research for our upcoming TV show *Animals, Animals, and More Animals*. Human interest, amazing pet tales, animabilia, that sort of thing. We thought SCAM would be a great source of interesting stories."

"I suppose it would. But I'm a little busy this morning. I've got a stressed-out dove and a frog with a herpes simplex infection."

"Really? But how would a frog get herpes?"

"I wouldn't even guess."

"This won't take very long, Dr. Forme. We just need a few little anecdotes to spice up the program. We figured that a vet like yourself would have some great little stories to tell."

"I'm sorry, but tomorrow, after the SCAM Ball, would be a much better time."

"We're taping tomorrow."

"Why don't you contact Laurie Delbingo? She's here this year. She has an adorable little white Shetland pony and a bunch of other animals. I'm sure she can give you some interesting stories."

"What about Henry Baldo?" you ask casually, trying to sneak the key question in on the sly.

"What about him? He never used any animals."

"No?"

"Didn't like them. In fact, I told Calvin when he called—"

"Who called?"

"Calvin Quinz. It's his frog. He was checking up on the frog and I told him that if the police think somebody killed Baldini they should *chercher le lapin*."

"How's that?"

"Look for the rabbit. Lepus cuniculus. Baldini was fatally allergic to rabbits."

"How do you know that?"

"He got sick at one of the conventions. There was no doctor around, so I went up to take a look at him. He could hardly breathe. It turned out that the previous occupant had kept a rabbit in the room. The ambient dander was enough to give Baldini a severe asthmatic attack."

"Let me get this straight. You think someone may have killed Baldini with rabbit dander?"

"It was just a joke. But when you think about it, it's not a bad idea. A rabbit would make a great hit man. Smart, mute, in this case lethal, and it would do the job for only a half cup of alfalfa."

"Who in the Society has a rabbit?"

"Lots of people. Everybody does the Hat Trick at one time or another. I think Terry Valentine may have one and one of the Melenettis, but I can't remember which. Oh, yes, and Mambo has one. I treated him for tularemia last year."

"Mambo?"

"No, his rabbit."

87

"Hello, who do you want?"

"Stan Eikenborn?"

"Why?"

"I want to ask him a few questions. Who is this?"

"This is Mike. What kind of questions?"

"I've been told there was an argument in your room last night."

"There's an argument *every* night in my room, pal. That's because Ike is a selfish, egotistical, self-centered little geek."

"Who is Ike?"

"Eikenborn. Stan Eikenborn. He's Ike."

"And your name is . . ."

"I told you, Mike."

"Mike what?"

"Mike nothing. Who did you say you were?"

"My name's Snoupe from hotel security," you say, quickly pulling out a new identity. "About that argument last night . . . the name Baldini came up, didn't it?"

"Hey, what is this? An inquisition? Can't a guy and his dummy have a fight without the whole world poking their noses in it?"

"Did the name Baldini come up or not?"

"Baldini? Sure it did. Yeah, that's right. Ike mentioned something about trying to *kill* Baldini! Sure, that's it. He hated Baldini and he finally murdered him. Send him up the river where he belongs...give me that phone! Shut up, you geek! That's enough, give me that phone!"

"Hello?"

The confusion at the other end of the line soon collapses into an incoherent battle of voices.

"Hello?" you say meekly when the struggle has ended and silence reigns.

"Please excuse my associate," says a new voice on the line, straining with restraint. "I'm afraid he's been having a difficult few days."

"Who is *this*?"

"This is Stan Eikenborn. Known professionally as Ike the Ventriloquist."

You are beginning to get an uneasy feeling about all that has preceded.

"All that business about me wanting to kill Baldini was just Mike's little joke. He must have his little joke."

"Mike is your..."

"Dummy, yes. But you see he has quite a strong personality and doesn't always behave himself. He always has his little joke on me, doesn't he?"

"I understand," you say carefully, trying not to further upset the schizo.

"Our argument last night had nothing to do with Mr. Baldini, nothing whatsoever. I never met the man."

"People who overheard your conversation said that his name was mentioned."

"No, no. What they probably heard was 'bald ninny.' It is a name I occasionally use for Mike when he upsets me. You see I created him entirely without hair, for the comic effect. *You* create *me*? That's a joke, you miserable cretin! You couldn't create a decent pile of turd!"

"Mr. Eikenborn?"

"Shut up, you ungrateful chunk of wood. Where would you be without me writing the jokes and signing the checks? Where would I be? Where I belong, you toad, in Vegas! Of course he killed Baldini. Put him away, back where he belongs, in the funny farm. It's back to the funny farm with you, Ike!"

"Uh-oh."

"Shut up, shut up! I'll never go back, never! I'll turn you into toothpicks first. I'll kill you, you bald ninny! Don't threaten me, Eikenborn, you geek. Two can play that game. Says you. Says you. Says you . . ."

"Thank you very much," you say melodiously as you hang up the receiver and leave the madman to his personal mayhem.

91

"This is the county coroner calling, Dr. Willis," you say, trying to sound authentic.

"How did you know I was a doctor?"

"Aren't you?"

"I try to keep that fact somewhat under wraps when I'm away from my office."

"Why?"

"People expect too much from you when they find out you're a doctor. Suddenly everyone's got ailments instead of anecdotes. But since you've found out, what can I do for you?"

"Were you involved in any way with the accident this morning?"

"Peripherally. The theatre manager called and asked me to come down to the auditorium to see if I could save the poor fellow. I couldn't."

"What did you find when you got down there?"

"They had pulled him—Baldini—out of this large water-filled trunk. Someone was trying to resuscitate him. I took over, but it was too late. He had taken in too much water."

"In your opinion, what caused his death?"

"I'm not signing any death certificate. I was just helping out."

"This investigation is strictly informal, doctor. We just want to close up the file."

"In that case, I would say he drowned. Pure and simple."

"But what would have caused it?"

"Locking yourself in a box under half a ton of water, that might do the trick."

"But that *was* the trick. Baldini should have gotten out in time. Do you have any idea why he didn't?"

"None. These fancy escape stunts are dangerous. Everyone knows that. In spite of the fact that it's a trick, it involves tremendous exertion, stamina, and strength. Many things can go wrong. Did you perform the post?"

"What post?"

"The postmortem. The autopsy. You are a coroner, aren't you?"

"Actually, I'm just his assistant. I'm gathering information. He'll fire me if I don't get it right."

"Well, just tell him what I said. A lot of things can go wrong. If Baldini got dizzy or confused or had trouble with any aspect of the escape, he could have lost control of his breathing and drowned. There *was* evidence of a struggle."

"How do you know that?"

"Bruises on his arms, cuts on his fingers, a laceration on his right temple. Like he was frantically trying to get out."

"Thanks, doc. I'll tell my boss, Dr. Jekyll, everything you've said."

"Which coroner was that?"

93

"Yeah?"

"Aladdin?"

"Yeah."

"Police."

"Yeah?"

"Questions."

"About?"

"Baldini."

"Shoot."

"All right, wise guy, what say we branch out into whole sentences."

"That's fine with me. I've got nothing to hide."

"Don't you now? We've got reason to believe that you had a gripe against the dearly departed."

"Harlan Kellogg tell you that?"

"Maybe."

"Gripe? I found that fat slob performing the Vanishing Sausage on my wife! You bet I had a gripe."

"Performing the Vanishing Sausage. What's that supposed to mean?"

"Use your imagination."

"I see."

"Of all people to go and have an affair with, too. Baldini! I didn't know whether to beat him to a pulp or slice him into bacon."

"Which did you do?"

"Neither. I had Madame X throw a curse on him."

"Are you serious?"

"You bet I am. I believe in that crap. For forty bucks she stuck some pins in a photograph and promised that he would never screw around with my wife again. And she was right, too. Best forty clams I ever spent."

"Amy Curtin, please."

"Speaking."

"Are you the stage assistant for SCAM?"

"Not exactly. I'm the stage assistant for the hotel. I work at all the conventions, not just SCAM."

"I represent the family of Henry Baldo. The Great Baldini. We're trying to get as much information as we can about the tragic accident. I'm sure you understand and would be willing to help us. Wouldn't you?"

"Sure I would. I saw it happen."

"You did?"

"Sort of."

"Go on. Anything you can tell us will be greatly appreciated."

"Mr. Baldini had rented the stage for seven o'clock this morning. A lot of the magicians do that so they can practice their tricks before the Ball. There's a small fee and you get the stage, in private, for a half hour. Mr. Baldini insisted that the auditorium be empty while he was rehearsing. Usually there are a few people around like me or Willy the custodian or my boss, Oscar Fore. But Mr. Baldini refused to pay for the time unless the room was completely empty. So everyone left. Sort of."

"Sort of?"

"Well...I know I shouldn't have done it, but I couldn't resist taking a peek at what he was doing. So I left by the rear door and sneaked onto the lighting scaffold over the stage. I watched the whole thing from directly above."

"And what, exactly, did you see?"

"The props were all on stage. A canvas bag, a big wooden box, a bigger metal box, a movable curtain, and a hoist. Plus some ropes and things. Baldini and his assistant went through the performance just like they would if there was an audience. His assistant tied him in the bag, then had him hoisted into the wooden box and tied that up, then put the box into the metal trunk and closed it with padlocks."

"Wasn't there water involved, too?"

"They had already filled the metal trunk with water using the fire hose."

"And then?"

"The girl closed the curtain and waited outside, counting out loud. When she got to twenty, she pulled back the curtain and looked very upset. I guess she expected him to be out, but he wasn't. I kept watching because I wasn't sure if it was part of the act or not."

"And then?"

"She took off all the padlocks, removed the lid from the trunk, and brought the hoist over to pull the crate out. But it wasn't necessary. I could see that right away."

"Why wasn't it necessary?"

"Because Mr. Baldini was floating in the water. He looked kind of...well...dead. She tried to lift him out, but she couldn't. He was sort of a big person. Then she started screaming and I ran down and Oscar Fore came in. And I think Willy came back in, too. It was pretty confusing. They sent for Hilton Willis, but it was too late."

"Who?"

"Dr. Willis. He's an amateur magician in the Society, but he's also a doctor."

"Now, Amy, I want you to think very carefully before you answer the next question. It's important. Would it have been possible for anyone to get near that stage or near the props while they were going through the rehearsal?"

"No, I would have seen them. I had a bird's-eye view."

"Doesn't the stage have a trapdoor?"

"Not near where they were performing."

"You're positive no one else was around."

"Yes I am."

"And Baldini was floating in the water, outside the wooden crate?"

"Definitely. Is that important?"

"If I find out, I'll let you know."

97

"Did you know The Great Baldini?" you say bluntly, deciding to get right down to business.

"I knew him. So what?"

"So maybe you knew him well enough to murder him."

"How well do you have to know someone to do them in?"

"Tell me about handcuffs."

"You mean my trick cuffs? Where'd you see them? At Mandrake's?"

"Maybe."

"I've shown everybody down there my cuffs. Nobody can figure out the trick. In fact, it's worse for the escape artists than the others because they can't pick the lock."

"Why not?"

"The lock's fake. It doesn't work. What really releases the locking pin is a magnet inside the mechanism. The magnet is a small ball that rolls inside a tunnel. You have to tilt the cuffs so the ball rolls down the tunnel and comes in contact with the locking pin. That's the only way out. Do it fast enough and no one can see what's up. Looks like magic."

"Baldini used handcuffs in his Triple Escape."

"I heard."

"But he didn't get out of them this time," you say, and wait for a confession. It isn't true, but it seems a worthwhile fib.

"So what? You think I slipped phony cuffs on him?"

"Maybe."

"Just because he used to steal my drinks at the bar? I always knew it was him. He wasn't as quick as he thought he was."

"Is that the only reason you hated him?"

"Everyone hated him. It was a hobby down at Mandrake's. Like darts. All he ever did was brag about all the women he was screwing. A real bigmouth. But he never fooled around with *my* wife, you can be sure of that, or I *would* be a good suspect."

"And how do you know he never fooled around with your wife?"

"Because I'm not married."

"Do you mean to suggest, dear," Madame Pollidor says, her voice a perfect blend of shock and curiosity, "that you can actually prove that someone murdered The Great Baldini?"

"I think so."

"How exciting. Who do you think did it?"

"Harman Hoodle."

"Dr. Hoodoo? But why should he kill Baldini? There are so many others who hated Baldini for cavorting around with their wives."

"Plenty of people had reasons to hate Baldini. But Hoodle had a good one, too. Baldini stole a hundred and fifty thousand dollars from him."

"Good heavens. He really was a bit of the rat, wasn't he?"

"He sure was."

"But if Dr. Hoodoo was going to kill Baldini, why wait until the convention to do it? Surely there were other, more private moments that would have been better."

"No. The convention was the right time."

"Why?"

"Because the perfect murder is just like a good magic trick. It's based on something very simple, surrounded by a mass of diversions. The confusion when everyone moved into the hotel, Baldini's obsession with his props, the practice run without an audience—it all worked in Hoodoo's favor. And the complexity of the Triple Escape helped cover up the one thing on which the murder was based."

"What was that?"

"That Baldini was deathly allergic to rabbits. The fur gave him violent asthma."

"I've heard that, too. But I don't see how a wheeze can kill someone."

"Very simple. Baldini locked himself in a thick, airless canvas sack for at least four minutes during the first part of the Triple Escape. He had to wait until he was lowered into the crate, then position the hem of the sack, cut through it, wriggle out, and tie it up again. All in the tight confines of the wooden crate. It takes exertion, dexterity, concentration."

"So?"

"So suppose he was in the throes of a violent asthma attack during that time. Just imagine. He couldn't get air; he was dizzy, weak. He could hardly move. By the time he did cut through the hem, he was gasping, choking to death, scrambling for his life."

"A horrible image. Go on."

"By then the crate was inside the metal trunk and the water was rushing in. He should already have been outside the crate but he was confused, exhausted, and couldn't find the releases. In a final effort, he kicked out the trick panel of the crate and tried to wriggle free, but it was too late. He couldn't hold his breath under the water and he drowned."

"Good heavens. And you believe that Dr. Hoodoo somehow caused all this to happen?"

"I'm sure of it. Hoodoo had an associate of his, Ollie

Bemble, spill a glass of gin on that canvas sack as it was being brought into the hotel."

"I know Ollie. I can't believe he would have anything to do with a murder."

"I'm sure he had no idea what part he was playing. That's the beauty of the whole plan. Nobody except Hoodoo knew the true sequence of events. All he asked Ollie Bemble to do was spill a glass of gin on a canvas sack. Very innocent."

"And then?"

"Last night, Hoodoo borrowed a rabbit named Waldo from the magician called Merlin."

"Duke Melenetti."

"Exactly. Merlin didn't have any idea what was going on either. All *he* did was lend someone his rabbit. But this is a special rabbit. It's been trained for a trick to follow the smell of gin."

"I think I'm beginning to see what you're getting at."

"In the middle of the night, Hoodoo placed the rabbit at the air vent to the room where Baldini kept his props. The rabbit followed the smell of the gin to the canvas sack, crawled inside, and waited. In the morning, when everyone started moving the props, the rabbit just hopped away."

"And no one saw this rabbit in the prop room?"

"It was noticed, but no one made anything of it. Just an ordinary rabbit on the loose. Even the rabbit didn't know that it had planted the murder weapon. Its own dander."

"And the police wouldn't have put all this together because only Hoodoo knew the connections between a canvas sack, asthma, a glass of gin, and a rabbit."

"And the water used in the trick washed away any evidence of gin or rabbit fur. Like magic."

"It's quite a story. But what are you going to do about it? Call the police?"

"Wouldn't you?"

"I wouldn't be so quick to turn Hoodoo over to the police. He may have done the institution of marriage a great favor."

"It's still a crime."

"Yes, but won't it be rather difficult to prove? There isn't really any hard evidence, is there?"

"I guess not."

"Think it over before you act. You don't want to make a fool of yourself, after all."

Staring into the darkness of the hotel room and hoping for insight, you suddenly notice an ominous shadow under the gap of the door. The slit of light flickers as the figure shuffles back and forth in the hallway. Perhaps the murderer has come to take the decision out of your hands. "Not without a fight," you mumble as you leap to the doorknob and throw open the door. But there is no one there. The hall is empty. Except, that is, for a small furry brown rabbit sniffing at the carpet. It is Waldo, the murderer. But has he come to confess or simply to gloat? You pick him up, stroke his long ears, and take him back into the room. There, while Waldo nibbles gently on your fingertips, you try to decide whether to turn him over to the police for questioning or use him as a mascot for your next murder mystery. And is *Now You See It, Now You Die* a good title?

SOLUTION:
Solving the Mystery
in Only Ten Calls

1. SIMON PENN ... #62

Following up on Madame Pollidor's wise suggestion, you call Simon Penn to get an overview of the Triple Escape. Besides that description, Simon reiterates Madame Pollidor's other lead that another escape artist might have valuable information.

2. THE ELUSIVE STREIBNITZ or LE GRAND FANTÔME ... #19 or #15

There are two other escape artists clearly listed on the directory and a call to either one produces the same information: a method of undermining the trick, and the name of Baldini's assistant, who should have checked out the props used in the trick.

3. WENDY COFFIN ... #35

In describing the accident, Baldini's stage assistant suggests that things weren't exactly going according to plan. You also realize that Wendy would not have undermined the escape herself because she was clearly in love with Baldini. She does, however, give you a better lead in prop assistant Woody Beams.

4. WOODROW BEAMS . . . #34

Baldini's prop assistant describes the elaborate security around all of Baldini's props and suggests that no one could have tampered with them. The mention of an escaped rabbit found in the prop room that morning, however, should register at least as an interesting oddity.

5. OSCAR FORE . . . #05

A casual remark by Woody Beams should bring you to Oscar Fore, who, as theatre manager, might have additional details about the props. Oscar is full of leads, most of them false, but he does mention an incident in which someone spilled gin on Baldini's sack while it was being carried into the prop room.

6. LANDAU THE IMPOSSIBLE . . . #04

The previous call points to a third escape artist, Landau the Impossible, a fact not clear from the list of names itself. Landau does indeed fill in the third part of the Triple Escape, from a wooden crate, plus a method of sabotaging it. But his statement that Baldini was violently allergic to rabbits should ring an even louder bell.

7. DR. HOODOO . . . #12

Landau's mention of the secretive Dr. Hoodoo having piqued your interest, you reach his daughter and find a reasonable motive for the murder. Just to make things easier, she tells you directly whom to call next.

8. ELENA MELENETTI ... #36

In explaining in detail the connection between Baldini and Hoodoo, Elena makes the murder for revenge even more plausible. For further details, it makes perfect sense to call the only person involved in the bond episode that you haven't contacted yet: Ollie Bemble.

9. OLIVER BEMBLE ... #58

Ollie Bemble's dislocated conversation supplies one more key to the crime—that he was asked to spill the gin on Baldini's sack by Hoodoo. His brief mention of a gin-loving rabbit owned by the Duke should fit in nicely with earlier hints and lead directly to the next call.

10. MERLIN ... #61

The only Duke on the list is the magician called Merlin and with this call the three threads—gin, rabbit, and allergy—are tied together. Dr. Hoodoo got Ollie Bemble to spill gin on the sack that was the first part of the complex Triple Escape. He then borrowed Merlin's trained rabbit, Waldo, to follow the scent of the gin into the sack, knowing that the rabbit's dander would debilitate Baldini when he tried the trick the following day. An almost perfect murder, which you have cleverly unraveled. All that's left is a call back to Madame Pollidor at #99 to close the case.

About the Author

MURDER IN A LOCKED BOX is the second installment (after A CALL FOR MURDER) in ALAN ROBBINS's series of interactive mystery novels for Ballantine Books. Mr. Robbins is an award-winning graphic designer and writer. His most recent books include CUT AND CONSTRUCT YOUR OWN BRONTOSAURUS and the collections of brain-teasing mind games entitled PUZZICLES and MORE PUZZICLES.